**DO NOT REMOVE
CARDS FROM POCKET**

# THE WINTER RIDER

*BERRY FLEMING*

# The Winter Rider

SECOND CHANCE PRESS
SAG HARBOR, NEW YORK

Library of Congress Number: 89-62521
International Standard Book Number: 0-933256-76-0

Originally published by J. B. Lippincott, 1960

First republication 1990 by
SECOND CHANCE PRESS
Noyac Road
Sag Harbor, NY 11963

Manufactured in the United States of America

To
Lonnie and Lib,
for the mise en scène

May my children's roads all be fulfilled;
May they grow old;
May their roads reach all the way to Dawn Lake;
May their roads be fulfilled.

*——Zuñi Prayer*

# THE WINTER RIDER

# *ONE*

The bell in the rusty tower of the courthouse struck nine while one of the Cloud boys was filling the gas tank, Usry, I think, though I could still hardly tell them apart. I asked him about Thirty-two, largely to say something to somebody, feeling good, expansive in the fine sharp morning, the air smelling of rosin and pitch and turpentine from the pine forest all about, of damp from the green-black river out in it somewhere, of wood smoke from the stoves and fireplaces in the back streets. Old man Cloud was sitting in the sun beside a rack of oil cans watching us, watching everything, eyes hopping about in the shade of his black hat like birds in a thicket. Thirty-two was the sixty-mile straightaway to the coast and the nearest Air-Express stop I could find (Jasmine Island, outside of Waltonville); I hadn't been over it this time, what with finishing up the job and all. It crossed the big north-south highway at the corner there beyond the station sign.

Usry didn't answer right off for looking out at the weather-streaked wall of the great truck blubbering to a halt at the light, then he said, "I believe they're working on it. Ask papa. Papa, he wants to know about Thirty-two." I was just "he" and "him," had been from the first, though they must have known my name well enough; I ran an account there, and they knew everything anyhow. A little way of being independent, of showing you there were things you couldn't buy, things you couldn't just walk in and have, no matter how many old plantations you and your friends bought up with your new money, how many deer you shot and turkeys and quail. I had explained I was just a visitor, just roughing it in the guest house. "Mr. Dukes is in New York. The big house is closed." They didn't care, or pretended not to; I was one of "them" or I wouldn't have been visiting—disregarding my car and the retreads and the seventy-four thousand miles on the out-of-date speedometer.

The old man said there was a nine-mile detour other side of Rucker, they had a bridge out, but I could get through. "Folks are generally going round on Fourteen to—" cutting off to watch the truck and the kid in a long brown coat getting down spryly from the cab. She reached up for a pasteboard suitcase looped with cord, then up again for a canvas-covered violin case and up again for another one just like it (maybe a little smaller); then, the light going green, she lifted a chalky hand at the driver, turned her back on the thunderbursts and walked matter-of-factly up the apron to the Ladies. When she had disappeared he picked it up where he had dropped it. "Yulee and One-forty to Deenwood."

I said that made it a lot farther, didn't it? and he said sure do, leaving it with me.

I gave it up and went across the street to the Naylor Hotel and sent the telegram to Dukes junior I had been composing in my head. MANUSCRIPT OFF TO GRAHAM AIR EXPRESS THIS AFTERNOON HEARTIEST CONGRATULATIONS TO YOU BOTH LOVE JOHNS. Sassy, but I felt like a surgery convalescent the day food tastes like food again. Then I sent one to Graham at the magazine, a not-sassy one, remembering the trouble I had been; I added that the short copy was his and would he kindly send the long one up the street to Dukes? He would probably phone Tom Dukes to send for it himself but it would get there one way or another and it saved me an extra package. (I had a second carbon at the guest house, though I have never lost a manuscript in the mail in what the newspapers might call a long and checkered career.)

I stopped in the bank and got a hundred dollars, more than I needed but I've come to like the safe side, maybe always have. Young Baxley, counting it, said, "You're not leaving us, Mr. Johns? You're so citified," and I said not quite; I was going to the coast on business but I would be back tonight for a few days more. If I hadn't lived out of the South for so long I might have detailed it that I was in my best tweed and flannel because I planned to blow myself to a celebration of cocktails and broiled pompano among the expensive suntans at The West Green.

When I came out of the bank she was talking to the old man, standing six or eight feet away from him and looking like a kindly bear with the overcoat nearly to the concrete, front open, cloth belt dangling; it made her seem almost hunchbacked, stooping a little at him anyhow, straight yellow hair caught in a tail behind (by a red rubber band, I was to note). She turned toward me as I crossed the street and I noticed she was wearing some sort of loose blue wraparound dress that was either homemade or might have been, and the usual flats. I thought I had never seen a young person quite so cumbersome, so unappealing. But an even more unappealing picture pushed that one out of my mind; I suddenly knew what they were talking about as well as if I had been standing between them.

And sure enough, as I slipped under the wheel and tried to make my door catch without banging, the brown squirrel coatcollar appeared in the other window. I thought she was smiling but it may have been just the way her mouth was formed, the even white front teeth so large that unless she deliberately stretched her lips to cover them she might seem to be smiling, or at any rate intent and eager. I didn't look at her eyes because I am not one for picking up hitchhikers and I was putting together a fast lie about where I was going, but they seemed to give off a quiet pale color that reminded me of the blue of gooseberries we used to gather in the country when I was a boy; her face looked as long as a pony's.

Then I realized the old man knew where I was going and had undoubtedly posted her, and I caught sight, anyway, of the heavy cube of my neatly corded package on the seat and felt again the general benevolence its being there seemed to spread over my view of the world and everyone in it. I breathed a sigh and laid the violin cases, one after the other, on the back seat for her while she heaved in the suitcase and then herself, coming in headfirst with gathered coat wings like a martin into a gourd.

Beyond an offhand "Thanks" she didn't say anything, either then or as we rolled away, arranging herself briefly and familiarly as if in a satisfactory seat by the window of a crosscountry bus, folding her hands in the wide blue lap; I was the driver and presumably competent or the company wouldn't have hired me, and she turned her attention to the flat little sand-cast edge-of-the-forest town beyond the glass—two boys with earflaps, running, late for school, a colored woman brushing pine needles off the sidewalk with a homemade broom of sedge like the kind witches used to ride, a loosejointed wagon from the country with a load of wired lightwood fagots, and after a scattered settlement of gray cabins, the pines that were going to be with us all the way, an hour and a half, probably, with the detour.

She was obviously used to riding with strangers, knew the etiquette. Apparently conversation wasn't required or even expected for she sat there, just riding, comfortable, relaxed, as if she had paid for her ticket and had some cash left over. Once, a few miles out, she lifted a finger toward a large bird disappearing above the skinny trees and said buzzard. I said, "Hawk." I was no ornithologist but I was still Southerner enough to know a buzzard. And the silence returned; it wouldn't have surprised me if she had unrolled a pulpy comic book and started reading or taken out a paper bag of fruit. And not offered me any. Passing a miserable little clutch of houses called Belle Vista I began to wonder if she was silent waiting for me to start tossing out the menu of leading questions we adults are usually supposed to provide (complete with fond wistful nostalgic smile back toward the golden young) and I asked the first one that came to mind, "Are those violins you've got there?"

She said, "They're not sub machineguns," turning the bared front teeth on me like a white light.

She said it on one time level, not from youth to age; I guess that was what I liked about it. You get that way as your hair grays out a little and your coat pocket sags with a case of reading glasses. I said something like you can't tell nowadays. I thought she might go on with it but she didn't, turning back to the window and the woods and the weak January sunlight even now thinning out with the overcast. I started to say why two? but I didn't care.

I was glad it was developing I didn't have to make talk; didn't have to make attention, either, to the two-dimensional talk of the young. Most young people today are already accomplished bores, with their bland assumption that the rest of us envy them their newness; they are as patronizing as a Chamber of Commerce president to a mere artist. I have no children of my own but the nieces and nephews underfoot during the couple of days I took off for Christmas did nothing to change my view. "The only thing you kids can do better than I can," I had had a middle-ager say in my book (one of the spots Graham had penciled), "is run and dance and stay up all night." "And make love better." "That's what *you* think, Junior." Look here, Bill. Patiently. The people who are going to read this yarn are the proud mothers of American youth—and so forth and so forth. And out it went; with much else too; I haven't been stubborn with editors for many years. She was about the age of Graham's pair, I figured. Twenty-four or five. Graham, that distinguished man of letters who was running the book, or the biggest part of it, in his May, June, July issues and would be mailing out, possibly this week, a check for just about the same number of thousands, Miss, I thought, glancing at her pink ear, as you have had birthdays. It was a nice topic to muse about and I was glad she showed no sign of obtruding into the dream.

There were so many delectable paths and views and vistas to it I felt I could never exhaust the sweetness. I had had some modest successes, very modest, ten to fifteen thousand; a couple of stillborns too (one particularly still, *All the Month of March*, which, perhaps defiantly, I have always been partial to), though Dukes & Son seemed satisfied enough with the over-all, Son certainly. I had never had anything like this, with magazine publication contracted for and two movie companies calling in, Tom wrote me, for an advance look at the script and, they all agreed in whispers, a better than even chance at a book club, considering what we had and what looked like a lucky break in competition developing round the July date we were aiming at. Dukes senior, who I suspect had never read the others, never been able to wade through, had sat up half the night with this one, called me the next morning with mellifluent curses for the sleep I had made him lose, sent me down to the "shooting-box" in style to iron out the wrinkles Graham had pointed to, sent Tom down solicitously when the ironing seemed to be taking longer than they had planned, fixed it up with Graham for a two-week extension on the original deadline and then a one-week extension on the extension. I had overrun even that by three days, but it was all right; I talked to Graham on the phone, a brief, rather wintry, conversation. Have it on my desk, Bill, Thursday morning without fail. It'll be there.— And it would be. This was Wednesday, twenty-four hours to do it in; eight for the sixty miles to Waltonville and the rest for the rest.

And it was not only the financial angle, not only connecting at last after so many misses; somewhere high up in the East Seventies there would be a quite handsome woman with an expression on her face I should have given a royalty check to see. "You are through, Bill," angry at something else but meaning that too. "Finished. You simply don't have the—the what it takes." She really had a knack at infuriating me. Something about Little Magazine tastes on a mass-media talent. Livia.

Of course that wasn't the whole story behind our divorce but I don't believe What's-his-name would have seemed half so irresistible if I had hit the jack pot three years ago instead of now. We had had a house at Montargis before the war, happy years they seemed to look back on though there must have been plenty of seedlings of trouble, notably the one that I had failed to see for its very obviousness, that, having swapped another for me, she might one day swap me for still another. I used to smile at the fact that she pulled her paper matches off the left side of the swatch and I off the right, but it may have been more prophetic of our differences than funny. She had gone to school in Switzerland, had acquired a good deal of the European woman's simply expert feminineness; I had loved her for the way she stood, for her quiet hands, for the tilt she sometimes gave her chin, and for much less superficial things too of course. She lost a lot of that after we came back to Connecticut, or I thought so. It doesn't matter. I remember how different I felt about the early Italian paintings I saw in the Vatican from the ones transplanted to the Metropolitan; ours are possibly just as good but they had never meant anything to me. Maybe the fault was mine, both in the case of Giotto and of Livia; it doesn't matter. Our paths have never crossed and probably never will but I liked to think of her tripping over my success at every turn next summer and fall and winter—a petty craving but mine own.

I am not a fast driver. I wanted to get back to the plantation before dark because I don't much like night driving anyway and like it even less through this sort of desolation, but there was all the time in the world. My idea was to deliver the manuscript to the express office in Waltonville a little before eleven (the plane didn't leave until six-fifteen) and then turn the car over to the dealer to install the new muffler and tail pipe which one of the Cloud boys had warned me about; I thought I would get a haircut while he did the job, then I would drive out over the marshes, which at this time of year would stretch away to nothing like a Nebraska wheat field but violet-colored, to The West Green for my clean transparent cocktails, my pompano, my down-the-nose survey of the svelte idleness, and a long relaxing stare at the Atlantic. I like to look at the sea, to "Seek it in the water wherein it sank of yore"— the "it" being, for me, whatever you had lost, or hadn't yet found to lose.

I should be back at the plantation before the plane left, having by then turned my eyes toward New York's Northern Lights glowing at the end of the shortest line I could draw to them.

I put the needle between fifty-five and sixty and held it there, the road streaking through the pines straightaway like the taper of a billiard cue, nothing on it whatever except now and then a scrawny small cow that took it into her head the grass was better on the other side; there weren't many and usually they stayed where they were.

It is flat country, grave and cheerless for all the green of the pines. The gradient, I have read somewhere, runs about a foot in half a mile. Every eight or ten miles the map shows a dot with a name beside it—Tarboro, New Lacy, Gardi, Rucker—but when you come to the dot it is two or three ash-colored houses, maybe a vintage gas pump, a few cans on a shelf inside a speckled window, and you are through it almost without noticing. And nowhere much when you are through it, one mile like the mile before, Odessa almost indistinguishable from Belle Vista. It made me think of time, not pressing time, just laid-out horizontal time, spans of time; not the time clicking away on my wrist.

Beyond a handful of sheds that once might have been a

turpentine still, I slowed down at the sight of a great hunch-backed shape moving out on to the black road a mile ahead; it was one of those Brahmany bulls you see down there sometimes, brought in from India to improve the strain, or maybe just to help it hold its own, used to loneliness and unfriendly pastures. I pointed. It always gave me a shock to see them, so far from home, so out of their own place, so peculiarly ancient on this new sea-floor land; you can almost hear the temple bell of another philosophy. As we went by he gazed away from us round his hump out over the flat wiregrass as if sniffing for a ghat or a stupa or a scent of the Ganges, alien to everything round him except the spans of indifferent time.

She scarcely glanced at him. Scarcely glanced, either, at the five feet of dead snake hanging over the road sign GARDI 5, though I backed up at the sight and crept past so slowly I could see the rattles move in a sleepy twitching, diamonds down his back, scales like a fish, a dirty winter-grass color—reminding me I was a long way from Fifth Avenue, reminding me I should be glad to get into crowds again. I am a city dweller, big city, where the dead, reptile, animal, or human, conveniently seem more or less to vanish; somebody attends to it, somebody else, like the heating of your apartment. And if someone you know is sick you don't droop much, or at all; there are too many people in your path not sick. The bell may toll for thee, but it tolls from so far away, round such firm masonry corners, you hardly hear it, deluding yourself but a delusion quite important to me. A snake over a road sign was too elemental for my taste, too close to the engine room. I had got the needle back almost to fifty-five when she said, "Is this your novel?" running a finger over my tight brown paper.

I must have given her a puzzled look because she added, "The old man said you were a story writer," putting story writer in quotes, watching me with the composed eyes, the big white teeth shining out like a pocket flashlight as if she were giving her lips a rest from stretching over them. You could feel her gaze like a cool air on your cheek, nothing self-conscious about it, just using it to take in what interested her. She lowered her eyes to a corner of the box and said, "William Wesley Johns," turning away to the windshield for an uncertain minute then shaking her head.

I wasn't surprised it meant nothing to her; I am used to that response. I said yes, I wrote novels, and she said, "The novel is no good as an art form." There were no possible grounds for supposing she had said anything else. She had small thin ears and a thin nose, quite long, with a pronounced bridge; her skin was the kind you see in cold countries, tinted, as if she had just come in out of the damp.

I said, "Well-ll," drawing it out, thinking I could afford to smile it off. It wasn't that such an idea had never occurred to me; in fact I should say the idea has occurred to me at about the mid-point of every novel I have ever written. But I didn't like her saying so; you don't like to have somebody disparage your car or your necktie though you may have had flashes of doubt about them yourself.

She added, "Except in Joyce. And he was really writing poetry."

I sidestepped it by asking if she liked poetry, a stupid question but most of the time in this life you are dealing with stupid people. She made it sound even stupider by repeating it. "Do I like poetry?" laughing with a puff of breath through her nose. "Poetry is a personality. You don't like all personalities."

I reminded her good-naturedly I hadn't asked if she liked *all* poetry, and she said, "Poetry is not a statement but an experience."

It was certainly not the talk I expected one hiked up

with a hitchhiker but I thought I would go along for a while; even if she was quoting her latest reading at me at least there had been reading, a phenomenon in itself. I don't read much poetry any more. I suppose it dosen't fit in with the sort of work I am interested in doing now. I asked her if she liked *Four Quartets*, the title coming to me because of the copy I had seen a few nights before in a shelf at the guest house; I hadn't taken it down but the very binding and shape of the book carried me back to other days—other times, other reading. I guess I planned on getting her out over her head in return for what she had said about novels.

She covered the front teeth for a minute, silent. I took it she was trying to touch bottom and let her suffer. Then she she said seriously, "Do you really like *Four Quartets*?"

I said I did and she said, "Eliot is too dogmatic. Poetry isn't philosophy." I let this sink in, then ventured there was Milton.

She flung out her wrists as if throwing down a hand of cards. "Oh Milton!"

I wondered if it wasn't a cover-up for having never read Milton but I said, "You're pretty dogmatic yourself, don't you think?"

"Shakespeare's the best one. *Take all my loves, my love, yea, take them all.* It's so simple if you know how," flattening her fingers, palms up, as you might tell somebody a culinary trick such as add a teaspoonful of water if it curdles and that will bring it back. "Shakespeare survives for his poetry. He's no good as a dramatist. Even Eugene O'Neill's better."

I asked her if she wrote poetry. You can't help being curious about somebody who comes out with that sort of thing. She said, "Oh no, I'm a fiddler," nodding at the back seat. Then, "I'm no good with a fiddle but I know what it *ought* to sound like. I know what the instrument will do. Which makes life harder," looking away with a brief smile. A black bird flapped its long wings off into the woods and she said, "Hawk?"

"Crow," I said, not sure at such a distance but meaning to sound sure. I half expected to be set straight on that too but I made it, maybe on account of the firm voice.

I don't know when we passed Gardi; before that, I think. Anyway, we were out on the billiard-cue road between the pines—roads, you might say: one through the windshield and the other, just like it, through the mirror, each with a nick of winter sky sitting on the end like the front sight on a rifle barrel—when I asked her if she was on her way home. The forlorn gray emptiness had set me thinking of crowds and chains of traffic and noise and the brownstone walkup in East Fifty-fourth Street I called home, wondering too if next week all that wouldn't send my memory fondly back to this.

She said, "Home!" in a tone that answered my question and I asked how her family felt about her way of traveling.

"Hitching? You don't have any trouble. When they stop you ask them where they're going and a few things; gives you a minute to size them up. The small ones don't stop. They're self-centered, cramped" (pulling in her elbows); "not big. The ones that stop are warm, open, outgoing, confident people. Once I was standing up at a crossroads in Jersey going to Providence. It was raining buckets. A man picked me up in an open Jeep. He had a waterproof coat on and a sou'wester. I just had this coat. We drove through the rainstorm hellbent for the Holland Tunnel talking about boats. He built boats in Bridgeport. It was one of the best hitches I ever had. A warm, outgoing man."

She sighed at the memory that certainly must have improved with time and clenched her fist. "I'd like to be warm and outgoing."

I laughed. "I'd say you were warm and outgoing."

"No I'm not. I just go round scared and trying not to show it and pulling my lip. I don't know what's the matter with me. I'm a mess.—Do you want me to get out?"

I said, "Here?" and she grinned at the wasteland. "He was a very fine driver. The ones that stop almost always are. Fast. Not reckless but knowing how, knowing what the instrument will do. You—"

She glanced at me, pausing, and I noted my modest fifty-five and braced myself.

"You didn't stop, and you didn't not stop. Maybe you're neither one nor the other. You got yourself trapped because you couldn't think your way out of it fast enough," drawing her breath in through her teeth in a kind of inverted laugh.

I said, "You don't need a palm to read?"

"Maybe you fall somewhere in between. You could go either way," breaking into a laugh that was pleasant enough in sound but curiously irritating in its feel. I suppose I didn't like the nearness to Little Magazine tastes on a mass-media talent; and it was too personal for my money anyhow. I fended it off by managing to say I was glad to give her a lift and she dropped it and started telling me about "getting axed" from the Columbia Symphony where she had played viola. "S.C., not CBS." I said something about one of these was a viola then, and she frowned at my slowness to comprehend (or maybe at "things") and in a minute, "I play violin too, but viola's my instrument."

The "axing," however, was what struck a bell in me and I began to wonder what sort of figure I would go along with if she was broke and leading up to suggesting a little loan, quote unquote; not now but leaning back in the window from the concrete of the next big crossroad, probably the Coastal Highway, the triangular smile gone wistful. I guessed a warm, outgoing man would hand her ten dollars and a small, cramped man would say he only had enough to get home on himself. According to her view of me I ought to say five, and I had to admit that five did seem about right. I said, "What are you planning to do now?" and she said no trouble at all. "God loves viola players, there are so few of us. Everybody wants to play first fiddle." She had landed a fill-in job at a restort hotel on the coast. "Quintet. Piano, couple of violins, sax, drums. They were short a violin."

I glanced with a sudden premonition at her pink ear and she said it. "Some honky they call The West Green."

It made me want a cigarette. I am a snob. I don't know where I picked it up; my father wasn't, nor my mother; pretensions don't get you very far in a small town. Maybe it's something you catch from living outside your provenance. Anyway, she wasn't the companion I pictured myself arriving at The West Green with. Which brought up complications as to how I was going to get rid of her, and where, and whether she and I might not in any case, wherever and however I dropped her, find ourselves facing each other at lunch across fiddle and pompano.

I shook out a cigarette, pointed it at her, which she declined with a never use them, and took it myself. Then I noticed a fog on the windshield though the sun was still weakly shining and when I reached over to press in the lighter I saw that the temperature needle was over on the far side of the red. I stared at it with all the symptoms of stupidity, waiting blank-minded for some directive to come through, the smell of hot metal suddenly rising full grown out of the faint whiffs I had been denying. Then drifts of blue smoke or steam or both began to seep up through the floor and I said hey, what the hell! and cut the ignition. The motor continued to run and I cut it back on then off again then on, the signals as bewildering to me as the first stutterings of a heart attack. I braked to a stop on the sandy grazed-over shoulder.

She was out one door as quickly as I was out the other. I turned to dive back for the box of manuscript, saw it bundled in her arms with the two fiddle cases and grabbed the handle of her suitcase instead. I expected flames but I didn't see any. The thick smell of burned oil and hot paint continued to rise up even after the motor floundered and quit; in the silence the radiator was purring like a big cat.

I set the suitcase on the black road and waited. There was nothing to do but wait; I had no extinguisher. I remembered something about sand for putting out a fire, and there was sand enough, for sure, if I could have devised something to shovel it with, which at that moment I couldn't. I cautiously raised the hood, freed a hoodful of smoke-steam, but there was no flame. As the smoke blew away I leaned over the radiator. I didn't expect to see anything that made sense to me; I don't know a distributor from a water pump. Except for the heat in my face and the burned smell, everything seemed normal enough until I saw her pointing the callus on one of her fingertips at where the fanbelt had been.

She said, "You got another belt?"

It was useless to waste breath answering that and I just stood there on the khaki-colored grass glaring at the steam and the smell, my exasperated fists on my hipbones, trying to fix some blame on somebody, even if all else failed on

24

myself. Why didn't one of the Cloud boys tell me it was wearing thin? Or the man I bought the battery from in White Plains? Why didn't I see it myself? Or maybe there was nothing to see; maybe it just went. Nobody to blame. The short circuit that sets your house on fire, the ankle twist that lands you under the wheel of the truck. I noticed the cigarette was still in my mouth and I threw it away like a rock. It had probably been less than sixty seconds ago that I was about to light it but it seemed to be in another life; I could hardly remember back across the chasm. And I seemed scarcely more awake to the present, gazing at the hot metal in a kind of stupor, then gazing up the billiard-cue rifle-barrel road one empty way then the other. There were no cows on it any more, not a pig, nothing, not even a curve to offer an illusion something might be beyond it, and I turned back to the bubbling black ambiguities under the hood. Beside them rose the red-brown fiddle cases, my yellow-brown parcel and the pale blue front of the wrap-around dress. A few hemp-colored strands of hair hung down over her high forehead and she was smiling at the tubes and pipes and cables, or might have been—the teeth were there. She said, "I know how it goes on if you've got one. Truckers always carry a spare."

I felt driven toward the senseless petulance of saying I wasn't a trucker, but managed to hold it to a shake of the head. She laid my box down on the worn stubble and propped the fiddles on top of it (I am sure it never occurred to her to do it the other way round), wisps of hair blowing out on the damp wind that still had a smell of night in it. When she straightened up she leaned on the fender for a minute. "This doesn't ground you, you know."

My face must have said why the hell didn't it? because she went on, "It'll cool off in a couple of hours with this wind and you can fill it with water and go on a little farther."

I said, "What water?" before I thought and she waved apologetically at the drain ditches full of yesterday's green rain. I said, "What's the use of that? It'll boil right out."

"You might hit a station."

I said there'd be somebody along in a few minutes. "There always is."

She laughed. "Maybe a buzzard," looking up at the overcast. "Maybe a hawk or a crow."

I ignored it. The situation didn't amuse me. I remembered losing the paddle of a canoe once about sunset on a cold mountain lake in North Carolina and the sudden change of everything from positive to negative. Fill it with water and go on three or four miles until it boiled out, then fill it again and go on—dipping rainwater out of a ditch (with what, for instance?) until you had filled it, three or four gallons as I recalled, perhaps more. And letting it cool in between or you got a cracked cylinder block, I knew that much.

My eye fell on a road sign a hundred yards or so back and I turned away without explaining and wandered up the blacktop to read it; I thought if it showed a mile or two to the next settlement I would go on and walk it and not wait for somebody to pass. If there should be no one there with the right belt at least there would be some way of phoning old man Cloud—the thought of him combining like a chemical with the memory of having met hardly a car since Naylor, maybe two, no more than three, and reproducing the words and tone of his "folks are generally going round on Fourteen to Yulee." I might have answered her with the same affirmation even if I had remembered the detour; she had made me want to come up with some

26

sort of proposal. But I shouldn't have more than half believed it, which I had.

The chances of somebody coming by, I saw now, were really negligible. Literally negligible. It was one of those situations you got out of by yourself, your brain or muscle or luck or whatever you carried with you; not desperate of course, not dangerous. Not even very uncomfortable. There was a chill in the wind and the over-all sombre gray was heavy on the spirits but it was not too bad. Not too bad, but also clearly not in that usual category of civilized predicaments in which "help is on the way." Help, in all probability, was not on the way.

It is a strange feeling to walk along a road you have just a minute before been rolling over at fifty, to find yourself on foot in a landscape suddenly motionless, your eyes still remembering it in an indifferent blur of speed. Nothing has changed but a relationship; it is the same you, the same landscape, but something has shifted and you get a sensation of newness, newness often, for me, faintly hostile; of being, abruptly, somewhere else. I had noticed it before, stopping at a house to ask a direction or jacking up a wheel and touching the grains of sand that a minute earlier had been just a color; I remember a country churchyard in times gone by on a windy hill somewhere in Ohio with a lacy iron fence that became neglected and cheerless when we stopped. You feel a curious halting of everything, not just motion but sound and shape and position, everything that had been changing. Suddenly nothing is changing. You are almost ready to expect your watch has stopped. The general has become the specific; countryside has become a particular field, woods have become trees, fences posts—in this case split pine that had turned black in the weather and a couple of loose strands of barbed wire. Many of the posts had an old char about the bottoms. You get rid of weeds and brambles along a fence line by burning them in winter and I thought someone must have cultivated this piece once though a long time ago; there was no other sign of anybody caring. It was spotted with a scattering of young pines blowing in the brittle wiregrass, volunteers, the oldest maybe five feet. Beyond the field the woods began again in a black-green wall; a few rags of moss waved in the top of a dead tree back in it somewhere.

The sign said RUCKER 5, the "ER" almost gone from the paint's flaking off round three rusty holes, as if a pretty good shot had used it for a target. I hadn't walked five miles in years, never, I was sure, five miles in a strung line like that, the black ribbon getting to be a watery gray as it neared the watery gray nick on the horizon, and I stood there trying to remember how long it took to walk five miles, wondering how much longer it took on a lane that had no turning.

I suppose I saw her standing there by the car but I was thinking of the graceless miles; not many sounds could have startled me more than the long round viola tone. It broke into a swift scampering of notes and ended in part of a trill that must not have pleased her for she plucked a string a few times, twisted a peg with her fist and bowed the long tone again. She had planted herself on the sandy grass in the firm-footed stance of a virtuoso in a concert hall, intense, oblivious, taking the run this time with the incredible neatness of a scared mouse pattering across an attic floor. Possibly a hillbilly tune wouldn't have been so incongruous but this was something else, maybe Bach or something out of a cadenza from some concerto, the white-tie orchestra poised there waiting for the little loop at the trill end; I am not too familiar with those things. Whatever it was it made strange company to the pines and the wiregrass and the low balls of palmetto fronds and the old rainwater scumming over in the ditches.

I was annoyed at what had happened through no fault of mine, at being marooned there, washed up on this beach of no-place, at the prospect of a five-mile walk, to say nothing of the hours of delay, and I resented such nonchalance, such handing the situation over to me to get us out of, such aplomb. It was almost as if she had gone on her way without me, hitched another ride—J. S. Bach at the wheel. And while I gaped she moved her feet, her flatheeled tan shoes, under the tension of a run that crossed three strings and squirreled up among the delicate twigs of the high positions.

It seemed to bring me into her view and she broke off in the middle of a note and turning her back, the rectangular khaki back, pointed the bow at something off the road below. I thought of our buzzard-hawk-crow exchange and hated to look; I had seen enough of black birds. She drew a sort of trajectory low across the sky, showed me the teeth and called, "Telephone."

Telephone or electricity I wasn't sure, but wires of some kind were crossing a field beyond the car on uncertain-looking poles, and when I walked down to where they left the highway I could see, farther on, what looked like an opening in the trees. It was hardly a road, I saw when I reached it, more of a logging trail or a firebreak, except that it wasn't straight, a winding trace, muddy and black, wandering in among the old slashes on the pine trunks and disappearing. I didn't doubt the wires joined up with it though I couldn't see where. No house was visible but there seemed a good enough chance of one not too far in.

I couldn't help looking down at the shine on my best city shoes. But I could get them cleaned up again at the hotel; anyhow, what choice was there? The highway was as empty in both directions as a strip of desert, nothing on it but the car sitting there with the hood up like the wing of a crippled bird—a crippled buzzard.

My first idea was to lock the manuscript in the car. I hated to do it; I had been close to that box of paper for a long time (I used to take the second carbon to the movies with me when I went in to Naylor, on the chance of fire) and I didn't like the thought of being separated from it. But nine hundred pages of twenty-pound stock is nothing to take along on a walk, even a short one. Then I realized I wouldn't be locking the car, with the girl there waiting, and I had decided before I was halfway back that, whatever it weighed, the manuscript went with me; leaving it there I could easily imagine my young hitchhiker suggesting as brashly as she thumbed a ride that she read a few chapters while she waited—or read them without suggesting. Or perhaps worst of all, not suggesting and not reading.

"I'll see if I can use that phone in there," I said, picking up the box and brushing off the alien sand grains. The cord had got a damp stain on the bottom, which I was sorry about; I am a wrapper of immaculate parcels. "If anybody comes by blow the horn. I'll be back in a little while."

I looked off the road at the problem of how she could blow my horn without the keys (it was that model). I couldn't leave her the keys. After all, I didn't know anything about her; she might fill it with water and drive away —"Here are the keys."

I held out the little leather jacket but she didn't move to take it. She said, "I'm coming with you."

It was a complication I hadn't thought of. And didn't

like; I couldn't be bothered helping her over the mud and puddles, talking, listening, adjusting. I am a Southerner and I tried to say no in a nice way. "You don't have to do that," I said, then made it a little more positive out of consideration for her different background. "You'd better stay here."

She glanced round her as if at the concentration of silence and aloneness, swallowed and looked at me with the triangular smile. "I don't like it here."

I said heartily, "Why? Safe as a church. You'll be fine."

She waved the delicate bow in an encompassing gesture of explanation and I said I wouldn't be long.

"I don't like it," she said. "That's why I broke out the fiddle."

"What's the fiddle got to do with it?" I suppose my voice sounded harsh because she looked down at the thing in silence and I relented enough to add, "You fiddle when you 'don't like it'?"

"Certainly." She said it promptly, reprimanding obtuseness.

"I see."

"Music is courage. All art."

"I see."

It was too big for me to cope with at the moment and I kept my feet on the ground with the thought of telling her she could just fiddle around there then until I got back. I didn't say it, though; I didn't think she wanted my smile. And I was also realizing more and more clearly now that her presence there today was going to make a difference, which was no smiling matter. Now that the sailing wasn't quite so plain, alternatives and decisions were going to be involved for a while and she was going to have to be considered; dodging responsibilities all my life—not always success-

31

fully but persevering—here was one handed me before I saw it coming (though I wonder if I didn't really see it coming at Cloud's, trying to slip under the wheel and get away before she nabbed me, before the brown squirrel collar could appear in the window). Now I not only had to get out of this little predicament but do it in consultation. I remembered the nice thin thread of simplification and freedom wound in with my disturbance over Livia and the divorce; life became with the decree so much less of a—dichotomy is a fancy word but it is what I mean. And what I was back into now. Except for her I might have been halfway to the telephone by this time. I said, "Somebody has to wait here in case a car comes along."

She slapped the bow lightly on the skirt of the coat, smiling at the ground, saying nothing, the cooling metal beginning to ping. I thought for a second of playing one burden against the other and offering her the manuscript to read while she waited. Then I said, "Okay!"

It didn't matter. Nobody was coming along and she would have been on my mind anyhow.

She twirled a white cloth round the viola with the offhand affection of a mother with a familiar baby and laid it back in the case, tucked it in. I opened the door. "I'll lock it in the car," I said. "Lay it on the seat. Lay it on the floor."

When nothing happened I looked round at her and she shook her head with a toothy half-beseeching grin, watching my face. I said, "You mean you want to lug that thing with you?"

The grin spread over another couple of teeth and I said, "Not both of them?" She looked at the ground and nodded and I slammed the door and locked it. I said, "All right, but don't hand them to me when they begin to get heavy." The senselessness of it all exasperated me and all the talk and the delay. There was plenty of time; it was only quarter to ten, but you don't get to my age without finding out time has a way of wiggling through your fingers.

"How about the suitcase?" I said with a nasty clip, catching sight of it sitting on the blacktop where I had dropped it. "You want to take that too?" She shrugged the great shoulders and I tossed it in and relocked the door.

As I was lowering the hood she said, "I'd like a drink of water, please."

I banged it down and told her I was afraid I had overlooked bringing any water to drink. She accepted it with a nod, hoisting one case familiarly up under her arm and taking the other by the grip and waiting for me to start. I circled the car—I don't know why, hoping for some impossible last-minute reprieve I suppose—then we set off down the highway in silence and turned into the track, I in front, picking a zigzag course among the puddles.

# *TWO*

I was in no mood for tramping, no mood for wilderness, no mood for any of it. She had said she didn't like it (whatever the "it" she was thinking of) but I thought her attitude was a good deal more serene toward all this than mine. I have never been one for this horizontal land-and-water country, low-pitched not only in the sense of level but in the tone sense she might have used it, in fact, to me, like a bass string loosened to a slackness where it has no tone at all. No musical tone; some antediluvian noise maybe. For me there is something almost primeval about it, Mesozoic (if that was the Age of Reptiles), laced with ancient lingering mud-scents and shadows and streaks of damp that pull your submemories back into the early volumes of the book of life, back to bat-lizards and dinosaurs and pterodactyls and fernbrakes and the low-growing palms called cycads, the fauna having risen and fought and vanished, the ferns and palmettos there this morning as good as ever, unevolved, unaggressive, undestroyed. Not that the land is old, geologically old. It feels new enough out of mother sea, indeed, to have tales to tell if it had a consciousness to tell them with—an Ancient Mariner without his Coleridge. But a Mesozoic kind of land, dragging itself up out of the brackish water, half in, half out, bringing up on its moist flats its own slightly more up-to-date models of the prototypes, its crocodiles and snakes and frogs and turtles.

And for me there has always been in it another dimension too, a sort of biogenetic dimension, in which these geologic depths are recapitulated in the depths of the individual. I have often felt, in the midst of crossing these barrens, a sense of levels of consciousness in me reaching back into the "mesozoic" stages of the mind's history—a flash of uneasiness in a fog belt maybe, reaching back, if you could have traced it, into crawling, hopping, skimming fears and dreads contemporary with the ancestors of the turtle. I have always hurried through this country, like a boy, I suppose, running past a cemetery at night, as if it might throw out a paw to detain you. As, to all intents and purposes, it had now done.

Yet I couldn't put my finger on any specific thing that seemed especially forbidding. Burnt stumps, pines skinned up the sides in long chevrons for resin many seasons ago, an unhurried fox that stopped in the trail ahead to study us and moved on, birds that were strange to me, some of them long-legged waders, herons maybe, certainly not pterodactyls. The woods had a different character from those back round the plantation which is higher, a few leafless gums and oaks but mostly pines and tall without much girth from being crowded and reaching up out of the dimness. I guessed the place had been logged perhaps fifteen years ago; many rotted stubs about, black streaks of charred bark from an old fire, endless beds of the knee-high palmettos. No rise or fall anywhere of more than a foot or two.

The air around us was as still as sea depths under a gale; you thought the wind had stopped until you looked up at the surface swell of limbs and needles, or listened up. The murmur that came down seemed curiously loud, possibly because of the stillness underneath though I wondered if it might not have been actually loud, with the multitude of branches, the accumulation of so many whispers. It was the sort of place where a newcomer is an enemy, probably a revenue agent until he proves he's not, though at any rate it would have been hard to take us for that.

I looked round at her wondering what we *could* be taken for, a pale-faced hatless man of an age when Life Memberships are no longer a bargain, dressed for luncheon in the gay world (except for the black mud gathering over the shine of his shoes), and a plain young woman in a flapping khaki overcoat dragging a pair of fiddle cases. I hardly knew what to take myself for. If I looked like myself I didn't feel like him; indeed, before I knew what I was doing I had moved the box and read my name. I believe the idea in the back of my head was that I couldn't remember whether I had written it William or William Wesley (I never use the Wesley, except on a book—my mother's name, though there is nothing Freudian in my having dropped it for everyday; William and Bill seemed enough and more me, on the whole, than Wesley). The Wesley was there and I was glad of it; the place almost gave you the feeling of leaving part of yourself behind and it was pleasant to see all three of me.

She said, "Hush!"

She stopped and I stopped too and waited, listening, turning my head. I didn't hear anything except the surf-sound in the high limbs. She said she thought she had heard a car on the highway, but we were too deep in the woods to hear a car even if one passed, though we didn't seem to be any nearer a house than before, the wires and the trail winding on into the pines world without end. Beyond her toward the highway each separate tree seemed to have shifted about under the patches of gray sky until it fitted itself into a crack or split in the view, weaving a sort of pole curtain that you knew you could walk through but that you could no more see through than through a wall. And it was the same on either side and ahead, an unaccountable feeling of threshold about it, of leaving and entering. Unaccountable in that I should have expected surroundings so dim and monotonous to suggest more a feeling of standing still. Except that their very lack of statement might imply transition—the dull quarter-hour between shifting winds. Whatever the cause the highway felt hours behind us, as inaccessible as yesterday. I thought I saw a deer but the shape melted into the curtain like the car-sound she wasn't sure she had heard.

Then I heard it too, a soft buzzing, more like a continuous flow of traffic over a far-off bridge than a single car. And growing in volume until the whole dome was humming. I thought of bees swarming but winter wasn't the time. She lifted a finger and said, "F-sharp," as if for her own amusement, then in a minute we looked up at the underside of an ice-colored Navy blimp nosing through the lower strands of the overcast, the two threads of its mooring cables trailing back under it like spindly legs. I couldn't help trying to signal, not knowing what I wanted or expected and knowing all the time we were as invisible as insects under a trash pile anyway; maybe a natural reaction in the lost. She put her first two fingers against her teeth

37

and split the air with a whistle. And on it went, a porpoise completing a dive, back into the overcast without a ripple; taking something of us with it, something of me anyhow.

When I first caught sight of the sawdust pile through the trees I didn't know what it was, small patches and slivers of a dull yellow glow crosshatched almost out of existence by the trunks and lower limbs. I thought of a clearing full of weak sunlight and of course of the house I was aiming for; I even wondered how long it would take Cloud to get going, to make the trip. Then I saw what it was.

Closer, it was as forlorn as everything else, a broad-based cone flattened out and discolored by the weather but still rising up halfway to the treetops. It felt like a mountain in the midst of such flatness, reminded you of Mayan temples in the jungles of Yucatan, though I am not sure I thought of temples until after I saw the Indian. There were gray dead trees about the base where the sawdust had drifted out over the roots as the pile grew and choked them; one thin straight trunk rose out of the slope near the top, askew from the push like a Grünewald arrow in the yellow side of Saint Sebastian. At the peak was a broken black cross that had once held the end of the conveyor belt. But what it all said to me was that the road we had been following was nothing but a logging track and this was where it led, where it ended.

I was gazing at it blankly while my mind accepted this, walking on out of momentum, when without any sound at all a man appeared round the base of the cone, coming toward us down the soft trail riding sideways on a mule, an almost white mule, not a clean white, putty-colored. He was slouched over his crossed leg in a boneless lump looking down at the mule's colorless neck and I wondered how much of a start he would give when he saw us. But he must

38

have been watching us for some time (perhaps he heard the whistle) because he showed no surprise whatever, coming on at us without changing a muscle as if he intended to ride right past us. I thought he was a colored man though I knew there weren't many in that section, then he was close enough for me to see he was an Indian. I raised my hand, half as a greeting, half with some of the same feeling I had had when I hailed the blimp.

He nodded without speaking when I said good morning, not checking the mule, coming right on. The plowline reins under the mule's neck reminded me of the cables of the balloon and I thought I am going to grab them if this man tries to pass us by. "I want to find a telephone," I said. "I've got a busted fanbelt on my car back there," and he grunted whoa! at last, pulling up on the greasy ropes.

When he said nothing I thought he might not have understood me and I asked him if anybody lived back in there with a phone. "The wires," I explained, waving a finger at them, and seeing as I did so that they fell in a loose tangle into the fronds at the pole beyond.

"No phone in there," he said, not looking at us but over the mule's scanning ears at the trail. He was dressed mostly from an Army-surplus store, paratrooper boots and a sawed-off old overcoat like the one I had been handed at Fort Warren in 1918, a round-faced man but without the cheer you expect in the well fed; a few hairs at the corners of his upper lip but mostly hairless, though he didn't look fresh-shaven either.

I said, "Anybody with a car? If I could get back to Naylor I could find a belt." He thought a minute, gazing down at the girl, not at her face, at the fiddle cases maybe, or just at her being in this place. Then he said nobody lived in there but a fisherman on the river. I said didn't he have a car, the fisherman? but he shook his head.

"How does he get in and out?" I insisted, as if I thought I could prove he was wrong. He lifted his heel, fingering the reins, and said maybe there was an outboard.

I said, "Can you get to Naylor by the river?" I don't know why I said it; even if you could it would take far too long. I think I may have been half-consciously wanting to detain him, even him, just another human presence in the wilderness, hating to feel the ebb of having him leave. He didn't say anything and I asked how far it was to the river, watching his surprisingly narrow hands on the plowline and seeing for the first time the pistol in the parched holster inside the coat. He said not so far, and I said a mile?

"I reckon."

"What's his name, the fisherman?" I've always had a kindly respect for fishermen; their calling has such an ancient lineage. Usually they will help you if they can. But his only answer to that was a black-eyed look at my face, as direct as an aim, and then a decisive lifting the reins and I said quickly, a glimmer of hope rising in me, "Maybe you could take a message for me. Where are you going?"

He nodded grudgingly ahead of him and I said it a different way; these people are very sensitive to the way things are put and I had probably already been too inquisitive. "I mean are you going anywhere near a phone? I want to get word to Cloud's Service Station in Naylor to send me a fanbelt. They'll know what kind. They know me. My name is Johns," feeling the words drying up on my tongue as he kept up a slow shaking of his head, either that he wasn't going near a phone or declining the errand. I chose to assume the first and began searching my pockets for some paper to write the information on. "Maybe you'll meet somebody who can get to a phone. Just call collect. Cloud will put it on my bill."

I had left everything in my other coat, cards, paper; I didn't even have an old envelope, my unconscious having rushed at the idea, I suppose, that it was done with making notes for a while. I asked her if she had a scrap of paper, anything I could write on; but she hauled up out of the depths of her pockets everything except paper—pitchpipe, leather purse, lipstick, comb, a cylinder of rosin, rubber bands, a toothbrush. I got tired of looking, aware all the time, I guess, of the paper under my arm and seeing I was going to be forced to mutilate an inconspicuous corner. I turned it face down and gouged off an end of one of the flaps as neatly as possible and wrote down my name and a few key words.

He looked at it skeptically without moving when I held it up, then accepted it and stuffed it in an old musette bag with "US" on it; it disappeared with the finality of the balloon. "How do I find the fisherman?" I said.

He gave me the aimed look again. "Mister, why don't you don't bother Mr. Goolsby? He ain't bothering you."

I started explaining about the car again but he had already kicked the mule with the heel of the paratrooper boots.

I looked after him a minute then turned my head not to see him disappearing. Unappealing though he was, the place was emptier without him. But the woods had given and the woods had taken away, and my thoughts returned to myself and my quandaries circling over me like an inquest of buzzards. "Well, where does that leave us?" I said, to say something.

She said, "Nowhere," emphatically, making the sort of hissing sound that I remembered was a kind of laugh. There

41

was a nice color in her cheeks. I thought on the whole she was having a good time, always an irritating idea when you aren't, though I tried to tell myself how much worse it would have seemed if she had been complaining. And I believed, anyway, she was quick at changing course. "If the man has no phone," I said, "and no car—" I threw up my hands.

"Maybe he can do something. No use going back." She had moved past me while I was talking to the Indian and she started on down the trail, the cloth coat hanging from the mound of her shoulders, one russet case familiarly under her arm, the other in her hand. I followed her, staring at the half-dry graying paste of mud over her shoes.

The air seemed different on the other side of the sawdust pile, damper, and I thought you could smell the sticky banks of the river; there might have been a blue vapor over the undergrowth, one minute you thought so, the next you didn't. I was gazing at my watch, surprised it was not yet quite ten-thirty, when she said, "I know who you are now. You wrote *All the Month of March.*"

My eyes bored into her back with that throttled admiration and joy that a mother must feel for someone who announces he has talked with a long-lost child; a favorite child, maybe because long lost. Still I remembered to be guarded; I felt she was quite up to looking me in the face and saying it was lousy or stank or whatever the hep phrase is nowadays, possibly so much shit, in their irresponsible delight at finding a gentility left to smash. I grunted non-committally and she raised the hair on the back of my neck by saying, "That is a good book."

It is sweet enough to have a stranger like a book you like, even if it has come out of someone else's typewriter; for it to have come out of your own makes the announcement quite a stirring experience, changing the look of the world, the look of the someone. Her hair became more gold than yellow, her ungainly plodding walk became a forthright honest stride. I thanked her, adding in a mildly deprecating way, "You mean was." Then I couldn't help asking her where she had seen it; she was the only stranger I had ever met who had.

"I read it one weekend in the Smith College Library. Everybody else had gone to New Haven. I'd have gone too if anybody had asked me," giving the short hiss and adding after a minute, while I fitted it into derelict young Saturdays of my own in dormitories drained as if a dam had broken Friday afternoon, the pecking of a typewriter dripping down empty stairwells like rain in a rusted-out gutter, "I hope that one under your arm is as good."

I said comfortably I hoped so and she said, "What's the name of it?"

I had no intention of giving her the title; all of us liked it—*Love Me Little*—but I was pretty sure she wouldn't. I overlooked the question, getting back to the more solid ground of how good it was. "This one is already a hit," I said, offhand.

She looked over her shoulder with the diamond-shaped smile. "But is it as good?"

I said, "Why shouldn't it be?" her walk merely plodding again, the strides too long, a kind of loping that lifted her shoulders up and down, a walk more like her father's than her mother's, if I had had to guess. I said, "Do you know how many copies *March* sold?" (I hate these abbreviated titles but I didn't want to seem sentimental.)

She watched my face for a second in her bland way, the white teeth framed enigmatically in the diamond, and I said,

43

"Less than six thousand," changing my mind at the last instant about giving her the actual figure which was nearer half of that, on the lower side; it had been over ten years ago but I remembered the digits very well, as did Dukes & Son.

The teeth showed a little more and she gave her two-edged laugh. "What's that got to do with it?"

"Oh now, please!"

"I mean it."

I said, "When you write a book you want somebody to read it."

"Six thousand is a lot of somebodies. Two capacity houses at Carnegie Hall."

"That's different."

"But is it? Orpheus and Apollo."

I brought it back down to earth by tapping my package. "This one may go to a hundred Carnegie Halls. Two hundred."

The yellow hair-tassel waved from side to side in some sort of negative, disbelief I supposed (I had trouble believing it myself). I hoped we had come to the end of it; I am superstitious about bragging. But in a minute she said, "Is this one written in your own hand?"

I said of course not and she said, "I mean is it yours? You?" which made me feel a little foolish. I dodged behind saying she would have to read it next summer and see what she thought. I didn't want to go into describing it; I had no doubt that someone who approved *March* would not approve this one. And the other way round too, except the author, who loved them one and all.

She said, looking up at the surf-sound, "I want to be a really first-grade fiddler. Not virtuoso, I don't look the part, but first desk. First viloa in the Boston Symphony."

"I hope you make it."

"I won't sell for less."

I couldn't help smiling. It was young talk, but good to hear—or what we used to consider young talk in the days before disillusion was in such high repute. I may have said as much myself; in fact I remember purple cinders on an icy sidewalk and telling somebody (Jim Crockett it must have been—at Chapel Hill now, head of the History Department) all I asked of life was to write one good book. I was glad if being young hadn't changed as much as I had feared. Except that I didn't enjoy her implication. "Sometimes," I said, "you compromise on a small point to gain a big one," sounding more on the defensive than I felt. You don't have to defend a successful job.

"A person always tells himself that."

"Sometimes you can swap a pawn for a bishop."

"I know. The cal-cu-lated risk," tumbling her forearm in a scornful shove. "I don't believe in it. The most important part of you lives on the level above calculation."

It was all pretty far off the ground but I didn't have the heart to say, or the nerve, "You just wait, Sister!" rolling up my sleeve to a scar or two. Still you have to say something after a remark like that. If you aren't going to pick it up, and I had been out of Hollis Hall a little too long to pick it up, you need somehow to suggest you don't deign to. I couldn't quite place where she had read it but I wanted to show I knew it wasn't a brand-new idea and I said, "You mean There's a divinity that shapes our ends Rough-hew them how we will?" not going into the fact that the last time I heard that had been under the narrowed old smile of Dean Few discussing the inheritance of acquired characteristics and using it to shatter a trap set for him by one

45

of the smarter Alecs in the class who had brought up the instance of circumcision.

I didn't wait for her to come in with some objection that might have led us off into other depths but tried to steer the talk back to the here and now by mentioning that she knew my name but I didn't know hers.

She said, "Should you?" coolly, possibly not liking my downward drag, and possibly also, it suddenly occurred to me, seeing in me a kinship with other males who had crowded her. I said, "Well, I'll probably need to call you something before we get to the Atlantic Ocean." She looked over her shoulder with a laugh and said I'd probably want to call her all sorts of things before then. "You can call me Jo. To begin with."

She may have thought I was smiling at her prediction. I was really trying not to smile at the name. It seemed so pat; not Josephine, or Josie even. A plain girl with a plain name. Some of the things she had been saying weren't so plain but I thought there was a good chance that, with names, we were back to earth now—a thought that had hardly entered my head before I heard her casual voice saying, "What is Man, Mr. Johns?" And when I couldn't believe my ears and begged her pardon she said, "What is Man?" putting a slight emphasis on the "is," and I said, "God Almighty, Jo!" and shifted the manuscript to the other arm. I thought it must have been thirty years since I had heard anything like that.

I had forgotten what the undergraduate reply used to be and I had had no recent need to try to formulate something more up-to-date. I didn't know how to respond. Having no answer was part of it but I also didn't know whether to turn it off as I had the other one or to gather myself up and try to face it. Because I could tell she wasn't just throwing it out as a stereotyped confounder. She, if you please, wanted to know. Unlike Pilate, she stayed for an answer.

I considered making a joke of it by asking if I had to say yes or no, but I had a feeling I had already used up a certain amount of the good opinions she had started out by having of me, that she was having an increasing number of reservations about me and my work, not to say my character. I enjoy people's esteem, almost anybody's, I am afraid. I know that some people's esteem is more informed and presumably more valuable that others' but I feel that esteem has an intrinsic weight of its own irrespective of whose it is; half a dozen little disesteems are likely to outweigh, for me, one big esteem. I hate to think how much I have paid in my time for the esteem of waiters and porters and taxi drivers. Of course Jo's esteem, at the moment, was both small and large—small, being a kid's (or so I liked to argue), but large, being the only one that was going to count for a while.

So there in the misty woods I racked through the dusty files of undergraduate sessions trying to lay hand on the way we had dealt with those things, trudging up the river in rain and shine, and down, and over the flat bridge in driving snow, and aching in twilights on the Common. The sets were available but the only old question I could resurrect on the spur of the moment was how a man could possibly bring himself to go to bed with a girl if he loved her, weighing it eagerly and earnestly, and loudly, with the subway trains crashing through the arguments. I am sure What is Man? was back in there somewhere, before the shorn lambs had been tempered to the wind, but I couldn't find it, only the sets and the dim awareness of being in a seedbed of integrity, very dim until you had had time to run into the lack of it.

I said, "Do you think we really need to know that?" falling back on a more recently developed attitude. "Aren't there many questions more pressing than that? Maybe not more important but more pressing. You have to take them up as they press in on you."

"Aren't you just trying to make it easy for yourself?"

I said I didn't think so (I wasn't too sure). "We don't have the instruments to deal with that one yet. But if we deal with all the ones we do have instruments to deal with and get them out of the way maybe we'll learn enough in the process to make instruments to deal with the ones we can't yet deal with."

"Such as?" the brevity of it a shock after my length.

"Well," I said, "such as getting the best brains in the country into the biggest problems." I knew she was going to say what were the biggest problems and she did, smiling at me as if she thought she had me floundering. I said government was a big problem, getting the best brains into governing us. "You *know* you'd better do that or you're a lost ball. Do that and maybe the next problem gets easier."

"Aren't you just looking for a shelf to put the big questions on while you write a bestseller?"

"I just think it's more sensible." I said, my neck getting a little stiff, "to go up a ladder one rung at a time istead of trying to make it in one glorious young jump." She looked over her shoulder to give me a patronizing laugh and I said, "You're pretty contemptuous of bestsellers but your man Shakespeare was a bestseller."

She said a bestseller was different then. "There weren't so many in the pit. Now it's all pit. And the only thing the pit can grasp is fornication. A bestseller now is just a manual of sexual techniques, just a How-to-do-it book. Millions buy it hoping they can pick up some idea that will make their next coupling less of a—sell." Her laugh was pitched at about the level of a viola, bursting out softly as if "sell" had been a surprise to her, as well as a delight.

There were lots of things I might have asked and added and amended but I am not used to discussing "fornication" with young ladies. It is a modern refinement of conversation I have no knack for. I don't mind writing about it and certainly a considerable number of young ladies will read what I have written, but I couldn't say the same things to their clear-eyed faces. Of course such reticence dates me but I don't concern myself much with that because, along the lines of what we had been saying, it is not one of my pressing questions; I have very little contact with people this age, find them tiresome and tiring, as I believe I have said.

But her words made me decidedly fidgety, first from having her skating so brashly on ice that, in my day, had been avoided (and with a charming delicacy) by girls able to draw on far greater resources of immorality, I was sure, than she; even Carlotta had never used such a word. The frontiers of seemliness have shifted, I suppose that's all it is. My other discomfort came from the feeling she gave me that I had practically wrapped my bestseller in tracing paper.

I was glad for the distraction of a whistling sound that I realized now I had been hearing for several seconds and taken to be bird song, very faint but coming closer and after a silence twittering on into elaborate variations on *"Possum Up a Gum Tree"* or one of those. She halted, searched about in the fogginess and crosshatching and pointed at a figure among the trees that seemed to be a man but quickly became a boy (closer than he had looked) with his shoes hung over his shoulder by the laces. He halted too, the whistling clipped short, standing there half hidden in the ferns and palmetto fronds, still as an alerted wild turkey.

Any human being held promise of deliverance, such was the point I had come to, and I was afraid if I moved he would break like a deer and run. But when, after a moment, I spoke to him he mumbled good morning, wary but confident too, studying one of us and then the other. His ragged hair reminded you of daguerreotypes of Civil War recruits. I started telling him about our predicament but he cut in almost at once. "You're revenuers, ain't you?"

"Of course not. I'm trying to find somebody with a phone. Or a car. I want somebody to go back to Naylor for me and—"

"What's that you got there in your hand?"

I told him it was a box of paper and he said, "What's that she's got?" I said, "That's a violin. Two of them." He obviously didn't believe me in either statement and hearing it in so many words like that I couldn't say I blamed him; it didn't sound possible and I thought it wouldn't have taken much to make me doubt it too. "Where do you live?" I said. "Do you live round here?"

He looked me in the eye, lips mashed together, refusing to answer, and I had to laugh in exasperation. I said, "Do we look like revenuers?"

"Could be you do."

"He's not a revenuer, Honey. He writes books. That's a book he's got. I play the fiddle. Look at this." She unzippered the cover of the larger one and he came from behind the palmettos far enough to gaze at the instrument, bare feet crusted with the chilled mud. He said, "Play something," and she smiled at him, reaching as casually for the bow as if we three had been dilly-dallying on a warm picnic with hours to kill.

I said, "Let's hold everything a minute now, for God's sake. We haven't got time for a recital. Has your daddy got a car?"

Neither of them seemed to hear me though of course they did, the boy watching the instrument as she lifted it out, brushed a nimble thumb across the strings. "Where do you live, Honey?" she said, twisting one of the pegs with that tight varnished small-animal squeak. He motioned with his shaggy head and said back yonder.

"What's your name?"

"Hervin."

"I'm Jo Seeley, Hervin." He said yes ma'am, he was Hervin Goolsby, then as I was waving at her to put the fiddle away he said, "Oh I reckon I can't stay," reminded of home I suppose. "My grandpa sent me after Dr. Luke," gazing all about among the pine trunks. She said, "Dr. Luke?" and he said, "Yes ma'am. He ain't home, I just been there. Can't find nobody there." He looked from her to me and asked both of us, "You ain't seen which way he went?"

I told him bitterly we hadn't seen anybody at all since we left Naylor. She recalled the Indian and I said, "Yes, an Indian." I asked him if somebody was sick.

"On a mule. That's him! That's Dr. Luke."

"The Indian?"

"Yes ma'am. Which way'd he go? I got to catch him. Sometime he goes all day."

I said you couldn't overtake somebody on a mule, but she said, "Maybe you can. If you hurry," and he set off, un-tying the shoes and tucking one under each arm and going into an easy run. She called, "Good-bye, Honey," which he paid no attention to, then smiled at me, starting to get the viola ready for bed again; "I figure Dr. Luke will spend at least fifteen minutes under the hood of our car, don't you think so?"

I didn't much like the thought but I had to admit it was possible, the "our" impressing me more than anything else, with its tacit suggestion of accepting entanglement that was a little like somebody hanging up his hat to stay a while. I wasn't sure I wouldn't have preferred "your"; it is so much easier to tangle than untangle. "The old man must be sick," I said, wondering what bearing that would have on our problem, but she said, "Not necessarily. Maybe Mrs. Goolsby's just having a new baby."

She was an argumentative sort of person; save the young from "insecurity" and they turn round and talk your right ear off. I said, "You see Dr. Luke as perhaps in gynecology?" She said obstetrics, laying the viola away in its crib, and I said, "Whatever his specialty there was something about the good doctor makes me glad he's not setting up to go to work on me."

She said he might know a lot of tricks, which I didn't doubt, though I wasn't thinking as generously as she was. She said, "These woods are probably full of all the medicines anybody needs. I've read of herbs that stop bleeding immediately. Some are anesthetics, some are poisons, some are contraceptives . All here in their own little truths whether anybody uses them or not."

I don't know what cosmic deduction she was heading toward. I cut her off. I had closer troubles if she hadn't.

I imagined the boy must have been within sight of the sawdust pile by then and I envied him coming to a clearing, dismal enough but a clearing, and coming before long to the highway. It made me wonder if we ought not to go back. I hadn't intended to come this far in, only to a house I had pictured just out of sight. It was still out of sight, and I knew now there was no telephone there anyway, and no car either, if I believed Dr. Luke. I wondered if the chance of help coming by the highway, slim enough, was not greater than the chance of extracting help out of this wilderness. Maybe we had better go back and simply wait. Or refill the radiator, which might have cooled by now, and go on (if the motor hadn't been damaged); we might get to Rucker before it boiled away. Refill it with rainwater from the ditches. Dipped up in something, maybe a hubcap, maybe the rubber floor covering in the trunk; I could find something.

My feelings were all urging me back and I tried to make allowance for that; I knew emotion could easily undermine some very good reasons for going on but I found it hard to examine reasons in the damp droning interminable cage, as hard as if the trees had been herbs and the wet-earth smell a paralyzing vapor. If the fisherman in there had a horse or a mule, what help would that be? Or if he had an outboard motor?

When I told her we were going back the blue eyes looked at me hard. "It can't be much farther."

"Not much farther to what!"

"We've come this far. There may be somebody where the boy lives can help us."

"If you look at it straight it's not very probable, is it? Somebody there is sick. Or having a baby, if you like." It also occurred to me that if we didn't watch out we'd be giving help instead of getting it, but I didn't want to say that to her; I suspected she had already filed me among the mean ones, "the ones that don't stop," and I didn't care about cultivating her disdain. It wasn't that I should have minded helping these people if the circumstances had been different; as it was I had no time to take on other people's troubles. "If they can't help us," she conceded, "then we'll go back to the car. And hope."

"We haven't got all day, you know."

"We're wasting time standing here." She hadn't so much as glanced toward the highway.

I said, "Go ahead," giving up. At least there would be another presence. My watch showed about five to eleven.

I couldn't refrain from adding up, as I followed her on into the unfolding and refolding obscurities, just how much time there really was. I didn't like to go into it because I was doing all I could and there was no use in agonizing about something I couldn't change. But looking at it, there seemed to be plenty of time. Figuring it backward from the other end, I thought if I had to I could take the manuscript direct to the field instead of to the express office in Walton-ville (troublesome but worth it if I was running close); if I delivered it there by six I thought they would accept it, maybe even a little later. I could do that if I got the car fixed as late as five. Allowing half an hour to put on the belt, more than enough I really believed, I ought to aim at getting back to the car with help about four-thirty. Certainly there was every reason to think that could be done. Until it got on to two or three o'clock I figured I had nothing to worry about; by that time some specific wheels should have started turning, as I was confident they would have. Several indeterminate distances entered into it that might change my figures a little: how far from the man of good will (if there was one to be found in this place) to the man of good tools? How far from the tools to the tooling? And perhaps other distances I couldn't foretell. But it looked all right.

The problem was becoming clearer to me and I felt better about it, glad now I had failed to turn us back. If the fisherman really had no car, as Dr. Indian said, he might have an outboard and for a fee, which luckily I could manage, would surely be willing to take us a few miles up or down the river to somebody who did have a car. After that the solution ought to open up very nicely.

I said, "Give me one of those fiddles, I'll carry it a while." But she shook her head. She said they weren't heavy.

# THREE

About quarter past eleven she said, "Anyhow, we're coming to a smell," and in a minute or two I saw a split-rail fence round a pigsty. On beyond it was a cabin on stilts, not very tall ones but stilts enough to remind you of riverbanks and rising waters, and beyond that, through the trees, some glossy black patches of a slow wide river. The cabin, the tree trunks and the water were all the same color—or colorlessness—different only in shine. And all the shines welcome. I was glad even for the menacing turmoil of the two or three long-tailed dogs.

But the first thing I think my eyes really focused on was the outboard motor, not a large one, rather small and hard used, but beautiful, lying over the stern of one of those square-end coffin-shaped "bateaus" they build in that country, propeller in the air. A whitehaired man with a thousand wrinkles in his face was squatting in the boat looking at us; he might have been seventy, eighty, it is hard to tell with these people, but he seemed hale enough, not in need of any doctor. He had evidently been doing something to the motor when the dogs started in.

He straightened up to study us with the scowl of someone roughly awakened, making no move to quiet the dogs,
one of which was inching closer under a trestle table packed
with a livid array of pint and quart jars of pickled snakes
and scorpions and frogs; one jar held a pale green rattle-
snake's head almost as big as my fist. I took up a stick,
which started a wilder yelping than before. There was no
use in trying to speak through such a din and we stood there
examining and being examined, the man facing us now, one
hand on the low gray side of the boat. Then without looking down he lifted a shotgun out of the bottom and laid it
crossways in front of him and shouted a word at the dogs
that turned off the racket like closing a faucet, a few drips,
then off. I dropped the stick in what I meant as a show of
faith but he left the gun where it was, saying nothing to us,
waiting. I had never been in that relation to a gun before,
not in front of it but just one step from being; it was like a
chessboard one move before being in check, except there
was no sense of play about it.

I ran through our story in a few words, calling him Mr.
Goolsby, which seemed to be right, the girl ahead of me, a
little to one side, as we had stopped, a pillar of motionless
khaki coat and a strip of ear and jaw neither pale nor flushed
and quite still, no tightened muscles working underneath. I
ended by asking if perhaps he had a car in which he could
take us to a telephone or a service station, speaking with a
false lightness at first, to no response, then with some of
the gravity I really felt, to no response, and concluding
with the almost abject appeal, "I have to catch a plane at
Jasmine Island at four" (exaggerating a little). There was
something baffling about it that reminded me of the hours
of trying to pick my way through the maddening labyrinth
of *All the Month of March* by my nerve threads years

ago—this way? no; that way? maybe? no—the labyrinth of difficulties and dangers of trying to make a reality out of the swarming nebula that is a man's potential self.

He let me finish then without hesitating flung up his wrist in a long-armed gesture. "Get out."

I glanced at the girl, the dogs yowling two or three times in a sort of echo then subsiding. My inclination was to accept it without protest and leave; we were really at too much of a disadvantage to do anything else. "Come on," I said.

She stepped backward, dangling the fiddle cases by the handles, then stopped with her feet apart and gave him the toothy smile she had given me back at the car asking me if she could bring the instruments. "Can I get a drink of water?" she said, nodding at a handpump in the yard by a corner of the porch.

It seemed to be a weighty question. He considered it for so long I mumbled at her again to come on, to hell with him. The pump was beyond the dogs anyway. And when I thought about it I didn't like the idea of her going in that much farther either; nobody could say I had invited her to come but since she was there I couldn't get away from feeling some responsibility for her. The old man might be harmless or he might be very dangerous, there was no way of telling at the moment. I said, "Come on, we're going back." Then he waved his arm at the pump and before I could tell her not to she was crossing the bare gray yard in her easy loping stride.

As she came closer one of the dogs lifted himself up from beneath the table as if he were being slowly inflated, each hair inflated, watched her without moving, tail hanging, until she leaned over without a qualm, used to dogs, and said hello, then backing away, jostling a table leg and sending an almost comic identical tremble through the alcohol in every jar. At the pump she propped the fiddle cases against a tree and took hold of the long iron S of the handle as if she knew what it was going to feel like. "We met Hervin back there," she said, nodding into the woods beyond the pigs, the smile saying cute kid. Then, reminded, she said she hoped nobody was sick.

The old man leaned on the sides of the boat without replying, studying her so doggedly from beneath the tan tufts of his eyebrows I began to wonder if he could be deaf, then he said, "Did he get hold of Luke?"

She explained it clearly and with a brevity that I admired, starting to pump, then stopping when the old man said, "Luke on his mule?" She said, "Yes sir," bringing up a strange little hint of home and family, saying "sir" to someone for no reason under the sun but his age.

Goolsby said, "He's gone for the day," voice falling. "Maybe for two-three."

"He didn't say," pumping in earnest now, a full stroke that suggested a childhood of orchards and livestock. The water table is close to the surface in that land and the pump started spouting almost at once. When she bent over to drink out of her hand Goolsby said, "Use the dipper," lifting a finger toward a weathered gourd in the low fork of the tree.

She drank out of it, spilling some over the spherical sides in her eagerness on to her dress. "Gosh, I was thinking I never would get another drink of water. You better grab some, Mr. Johns," clanking up another dipperful and holding it out, and dropping the whole thing as her eye fell on the dead man lying on the floor of the porch. One of the dogs jumped back with a yelp as the water splashed him. He was a redheaded man, some gray, about my age with a misty pink stubble on his cheeks, the top of his skull toward the steps as if he had been dragged out of the house by the shoulders. You could tell he was dead by the jut of his chin.

My response may have been less galvanic than hers but I think I went on responding after she had recovered herself. I heard her say, misunderstanding, "Somebody *is* sick then," turning the teeth and the blue eyes on old Goolsby in the boat while I was still unable to put anything into words, almost into thought; I couldn't get past the feeling we had walked into something not meant for us, though I knew I was an exaggerator, either by nature or from the miles of fiction behind me. But when you see a gun and a dead man you can't help leaving room for the possibility they fit together; I even held off looking at the boat as if that would prevent Goolsby from being alarmed. But there was no exaggeration about the redheaded man.

Goolsby didn't answer for several seconds then he said, "He's gone, ma'am," stressing the "gone" with a bitter show of offhandedness. She said oh!, looked back at the porch, then, "Is he dead?"

"Jared's gone, yes ma'am."

She said, "your son?" but I didn't see any use in going into that with all the other questions crowding up and I said, "What happened?"

"The Lord took him, that's what happened." I asked if there had been an accident and he said, "He had a seizure. Yesterday evening, trying to hist the motor out. I got him to bed, put the ax underneath to cut the pain and he seemed to be resting well. But this morning he was gone."

I gazed at the porch, thinking of myself, as you will. "He wasn't an old man."

"Old enough," he said with a kind of a snort. "You don't have to be old."

She said, "Oh I'm so sorry. The little boy didn't tell us."

"I didn't say anything to Hervin. Just sent him to get Luke."

I supposed it was all right; there was no reason to think it wasn't, no signs of any trouble. And it wasn't my business anyhow. You learn to mind your own business in New York, one of its most appealing aspects to me. But another angle of the thing was already taking shape in my head. Whatever the details, the old man had worries of his own; he wouldn't be putting them aside to help us, even if he could. It seemed to me there was nothing much we could do for him; our best interests lay in getting out, which was certainly my inclination too, and it occurred to me I might use the Indian as excuse, promise to search for him as we went back to the highway and send him in. I tried to catch Jo's eye to signal her we were leaving but she was still looking at the old man.

Goolsby said, "I wanted Luke to help me with him," gazing up the river then turning his little eyes on me.

I suppose the same thought occurred to all of us, mine complicated by another glimpse of my increasing suspicion that I should have been better off if I had left Jo cursing me from Cloud's concrete. Except for her I thought I might have got out of it by simply telling the truth: I had no time to spare (and I knew that without looking at my watch). Or maybe convincing him I shouldn't have been of any help to him anyhow by showing my indoor soft-muscled hands, or making a gesture at my clothes. Then I thought of something else. "You'll have to wait for Luke to sign papers anyway, won't you?"

"He'll take care of all that when he comes, don't matter when."

It was no surprise to me to hear her say, "We'll help

you," and I was ready with firmness. I said I was sorry but there just wasn't time, speaking to both of them. "We've got to get the car fixed and be on our way." I told Goolsby I was sure he would understand (I hate the phrase but it slipped out); I said I was in need of help too, of a less solemn kind, certainly, but perhaps even more pressing. I didn't go into when they filled out the papers; quite likely in these remote places they would shade the formalities. It was time that bothered me. And I suppose, to be honest, the fact that I didn't like the job. "Hervin will be back with Luke before long to help you," doubting it very much but saying so anyhow.

She had obviously stopped listening to me, standing solid with her feet apart, fists on her hips, waiting for the old man to say what he wanted done. I thought of turning away and starting back along the path alone; she would follow. Wouldn't she? And I wasn't at all sure she would. Well, suppose she didn't? Let her come or not; I hadn't asked for the responsibility of looking after her. Goolsby said, "I want to take Jared to the island."

She repeated, "Island?" and he said, "It's higher ground on the island." Then he said, gazing into the trees but clearly addressing me, "If you could have time to help me out I might could take you to a man's got a car."

This was too pat. I suspected he had made it up on the spur of the moment; it was the first indication he had given that he had heard a word of our story. I said, "Where does this man live?" thinking I might bring out whether he was deceiving me, conscious too of how it had all turned round now from his trying to get rid of us to trying to keep us.

"You couldn't find him."

I wanted to say was he sure *he* could? but I said, "In walking distance?"

"Take you all day to walk. No path through the woods."

I said, "How would I get there then?" and he nodded in front of him at the gun but meaning the boat. "I'd carry you."

I didn't like the terms but it was the only break so far in our deadlock on any terms (I believed now there was such a man, probably down the river somewhere). I thought of offering him some excessive amount of money that he couldn't refuse—fifty dollars, seventy-five—to take us now but I decided against it; he might already have guessed I had money in my pocket but such an offer as that might have made him realize he could have that and all the rest I had without taking us anywhere. I didn't know anything about him; all I knew was that an old man with a twelve-gauge is far from decrepit.

I said, "Couldn't you take us now? I'd be glad to pay you what you think is right."

He answered so promptly it was practically an interruption. "I don't want your money, Mister. None of it." And I saw what I should have seen before, that it wasn't reasonable to think he would leave the body. Jared lay right square between me and help; the only way to get help was first to bury Jared.

I looked back into the depths beyond the pigsty for some sign of the boy or the Indian and then I said all right, I'd help him, telling myself I had better accept the bargain, hoping blindly it was on the level, since as a matter of fact he could as easily have forced me to help him as to hand over my billfold.

He laid the gun in the bottom of the bateau, his lean face showing nothing, not relief or triumph or anything, and rose up into quite a tall figure and stepped familiarly over the two cross seats into the bow and out onto the black bank. He walked to a corner of the porch, bent over and got some tools from underneath among a scattering of Mason jars, a shovel, an ax and a short-handled spade, and I set the manuscript on the trestle table and took the tools and put them in the boat. Then he beckoned me with his chin and I followed him round the house to an entrance at the back into a sort of breezeway, up two or three steps. I didn't know what he had come for, still didn't know when I stood beside him gazing up with him at the open joists and the collection of fishing poles, nets, boxes, cases and indiscriminate litter piled across them. Then I saw what he wanted and I kept on looking at it while he got two cow-hide chairs out of the kitchen and placed them where we could stand on them and reach the beams. He said, "I got this for myself at the store in Rucker must be twelve years ago, give a nice shoat for it."

It was bottom-side up, on account of snakes and rats I suppose, weathered as dark as the old man's wrists by the heat and the damp, the lid not attached, leaning against it. We worked it down and he wiped it inside and out with a strip of burlap. He tore off a yellowed envelope fastened to the lid with carpet tacks and cast it on a table.

It made a heavy enough burden with the lid propped inside but we managed it, carried it to the boat and set it on the bank. I said, "That'll make a lot of weight in the boat, won't it?" adding it in my mind to the three of us, the four. But he didn't answer, taking out the lid and laying it lengthwise across the seats; then he beckoned me again with his stubbled chin and we went up the steps to the porch and lifted his redheaded son by the shoulders and bare feet and brought him down and over the yard, the thin hard ankles reminding me of the handles of some wheelbarrow I had pushed I couldn't say when but certainly not in forty years. We laid him out on the lid, the girl steadying the bow overhanging the bank as the stern settled and swayed with a spongy motion under the load.

He was the first dead man I think I had ever touched and on the porch I had shrunk like a child from laying my hand on him; indeed, I have no doubt this prospect had laced through most of my conscious reasons for dodging the job. I have city tastes, inherited or acquired I don't know, and I said to myself as I lifted him, all your life a fugitive from funerals and here at last in the very middle of one—well, not quite the very middle—as if, college-like, there are certain courses required of a man for a degree. But stumbling down the steps and over the tree roots and into the boat my feelings toward Jared changed a little and I found myself taking care as I laid down his feet to put his heels together in a seemly pose. He was clothed in washed-out denims, jacket and pants, nothing else I guessed, pale skin showing in long lozenges between the metal buttons. There was nothing pathetic about him, simple and gray and dignified as a fallen stone. His feet were clean, obviously newly bathed, and it sent me back to thinking of the old man's use of gone instead of dead, using it I now felt, less as a thin-skinned evasion than as a slight extra courtesy to the dead man, a more than slight respect for the state of death, as you might say supper instead of food or eats.

We waited in silence—I seemed to have nothing to say and neither did she—while Goolsby went back to the house again. He returned shortly with a length of plow-line looped over his forearm and a folded sheet with a black book on it that I knew was a Bible; he brought a hammer too in the same hand under the sheet and as he passed a tree grasped the shaft of a homemade weathered paddle leaning against it, the blade no wider than your palm, and came on at a thoughtful pace, using the paddle as a kind of staff and looking not so much like the bereaved father as like a guide who knows the way. He pulled the boat against the bank and laid what he carried on the seat by Jared's shoulder; it seemed as if, after all this, he was going to leave the coffin behind but when he drove a nail in the front and tied an end of the rope to it I realized what he was doing. "Buried papa the same way," he said, and we pushed it into the water. It floated out behind the bateau on the slow current like a frailer brother hand in hand with his elder.

Jo stepped across the seats into the stern as he directed and seated herself in a large khaki mound to one side of the motor.

I was on the narrow perch in the bow, swinging out beneath the overhanging branches when in a flush of panic I remembered the manuscript. I said, "Wait a minute! I forgot something," amazed I could have done so.

"I've got it," she said. And sure enough, straight back beyond the dead man's shoulder, beyond the pair of cases propped against her knees like twins that had grown at slightly different speeds, my brown box lay solidly in her lap under her crossed forearms. I nodded my thanks, which she didn't see, turning her eyes away from the body to sweep the opening reaches of the black river, the quiet shattered by the sudden catching of the motor.

It was certainly for me an unprecedented situation, would have been for most people, I should imagine, and I coudn't understand why it seemed no more strange than it did. My feeling was not the familiar paradox you sometimes notice of seeming to have lived a particular moment before. The moment was unlived enough, new enough, but it didn't draw your mind into the tight perplexity of facing the totally unfamiliar. And of course much of it was familiar—water, boat, youth, age, even death, the sense of minutes growing into hours; my memory could pick up a long chain of encounters with such things. Perhaps it was only the combination that was new, the proportions, an unfamiliar arrangement of familiar fragments, and that would account for the lack of strangeness. It was a little like arriving at some place you have read about or been told about; unexpected overlying expected. Maybe all I am trying to say is that my uneasiness was different from a general fear of the unknown, that there was enough of a tie-in somewhere that I couldn't trace to connect it with what I knew. I had never dug a man's grave before but I could remember the feel of a shovel.

The motor hadn't much power, pushing us doggedly out into the current, the water running high along the freeboard from the cargo we made, a thin 'foam rising at the bow of our pine-brown tender. The sight of open sky, a wide uneven band, sunless and gray, had a releasing effect on muscles I hadn't known were tight, heavy and overcast though it was. I had a feeling of having come through a door, through a shadow—shade it still was but not shadow —that reminded me of the way you felt passing through windowless cotton warehouses to the great door into the yard, back in the days of my shovel, I suppose, and the wheelbarrow. I turned and gazed at the girl's bright hair just to see something with color; her face seemed whiter than it had been but there remained a subdued red in her skin that made me think of the nice ambiguities of "sanguine," meaning red and meaning hope and confidence too. She was clearly not happy, but close beneath her unhappiness the color said she was in good heart, and the sight of it down the length of unsanguine Jared was heartening to the uneasiness in me too. The old man was sitting sideways in a loose-shouldered lump staring glassy-eyed into the cypresses and gum trees on the far bank, which seemed to be where we were headed.

I was thinking that the land in there appeared to be no higher that what we had left, island though it might have been—one of those strings of land you see on maps of that country, with a lagoon behind it or a thin current—when, getting out of the strong midstream, he swung us up the river, close along the shore, the moss drifting overhead like puffs of smoke. The water in here had an undertone of amber that gave it the color of weak coffee.

I wondered if the presence of the dead man there in front of her knees was what disturbed her. It might have disturbed me at her age, or in fact much later. Not now. I was surprised at how little difference it made in me. I often think about death now that I am older and without doubt coming measurably close (I use "older" because "old" gags me, though certainly I was, as the old man said of Jared, old enough); but you pass a point somewhere in your life where the sight of death ceases to remind you so much that you too will die, which you are quite conscious of, and reminds you more that you are living, which you sometimes forget. Your time is still running; get on with the job you set yourself. What the dead man said to me, peeping down at me over his cheekbones out of his almost closed eyes, was if you are any longer out to write one good book, Brother, get writing. Before the drowning Jareds pull you under.

No, I was unhappy on a much more constricted level. Length after length we were shoving up the river, and every length we would have to retrace. Every five minutes was really ten. I said, "How far up is this island?" wondering why I hadn't found out about that before I consented to come, though you didn't do much consenting with somebody who had a gun, pointed at you or not.

He nodded up ahead but when I looked I knew he had been just putting me off; up yonder was all he had said. The river reminded me of one of its white-gray bass packed in damp moss for taking home, the current with a scaly shine from the sky, and the woods moss itself not much different in color from the water. And low against it as we were, the bends were unpronounced and the water-space seemed enclosed like a lake; the current seemed to be flowing out of the woods ahead and back into the woods below.

Through the half-hearted motor-sounds I heard Jo asking him about the boy, what he would do about him, where his mother was. Goolsby spit over the side before he answered. "Mother's no good. Gone. Pulled up and went to Jax, five years ago, six. Last we heard of her." He said Hervin would be all right. "Hervin ain't a baby, ma'am. You think he's a nonny, but he knows a lot of things. Sar; h's been a mother to him."

ʃ ie said, "Sarah?" but he had his mind on other things. Or else the name returned him to Jared.

He said in a minute, "Jared was a good boy. He never took much to being a fisherman. Heart never in it. More than anything in the world, wanted to run a filling station. Waltonville, Naylor, Bluffton, all one to him long as it was a filling station." He went on, talking, not talking, I couldn't hear very well and didn't care; he was talking to her, not me, anyhow. Or talking to himself. I heard him say Jared was quite a hand with the girls, walk all the way to Rucker for a dance, and I couldn't help looking down at the clean-washed having-danced feet.

Ten days ago Jared took cold. "Got caught in a rainstorm on the river. Luke give him one of his simples.

Sweated him. Couple of days Jared's all right, weak but all right. Luke give him something to bring his strength back. It didn't help him, little or none."

She said, "I guess you'll be lonesome without Jared." He seemed to think about it for a while, then he said, "Lonesome?" as if he hadn't caught the word.

She said it would be too lonesome down there for her and he said, "Ain't ever heard anybody worried about lonesome but city people. Ain't anybody in the Bible was lonesome I ever heard of. Mr. Oglethorpe all over this country, if he was lonesome I ain't heard it."

I felt myself being swung away from the bank and saw that he was steering out into the swifter water and I thought he was crossing back to the other side for some reason of his own. I didn't guess that what looked like the other bank was the island until the noise of the motor suddenly disappeared into a cloud of silence, didn't know for sure until the low moss was brushing over my head.

It takes a good while for a grave if one of the gravediggers doesn't know how. We laid him on the wild grass of a slightly raised clearing not far from the boat where two or three overgrown mounds indicated a cemetery, chopped a line in the earth all round the coffin lid with the ax, moved him to one side and started digging. The air was damp and with no sun to warm it as joyless and chilled as early morning, but I was out of breath and sweating before we had dug away the weeds; I wasn't used to that sort of work, did it awkwardly with too many motions, was always in my own way. I could see the old man digging easily, one movement flowing on into the next, no breaks, no edges or corners, and with hardly a drop of sweat on his face; he dug deliberately, with a lack of urgency that I

70

thought he might be considering was a fitting attitude toward what we were doing but that irked me no less, time on my mind, until I noticed he had moved as much of the black earth at his end as I had at mine.

I hadn't taken off my coat, partly because of the chill (the wind had been following but getting out of the boat was like coming about into it and the bared woods round the clearing offered no sort of break) and partly because the old man still wore his thick sweater and I didn't want to seem lacking in decorum, but when he pulled off the sweater I did the same with my coat, my best Forty-fifth Street tweed coat, and folding it inside out laid it on the stiff grass. He left the loose sleeves of a dingy undershirt hanging about his forearms, but I went on and rolled up my cuffs to the elbow, largely with the idea of keeping them fresh, The West Green I suppose, dinner replacing lunch, still hovering in the back of my head.

I was lifting the worn grip of the spade again when I heard the soft plunks of the viola being tuned. It startled me as it had back on the highway, but it seemed to startle Goolsby a good deal more; he took his foot off the shovel blade, crossed his wrists as if permanently on the top of the handle and watched her. I returned to the digging, meaning it as a suggestion to him though he ignored it; I could feel a blister already beginning between my left thumb and finger and I should have been glad for a rest too but when I had put my wristwatch in my pocket I had seen it was nearly ten after twelve. The grave was only about a foot deep, a little more at his end.

From her "breaking out the fiddle" I guessed that her un-happiness had congealed, as before, into an undeniable pres-ence, though you might not have thought it came from the immediate conditions for she looked at neither of us, not at the body nor the coffin beside it, but, testing the four tones until she was satisfied, she wandered off a few steps toward the edge of the rise, running up and down the scale in oddly delicate little bursts as she walked, then facing dowr the river, she finished off with a long-bowed note on an open string that led somehow straight on into the beginning of something like "Sheep May Safely Graze."

I moved about in the soft black hole, making a show of my efforts, words forming in my mind from his rapt expression that I didn't quite dare say—shall we get on with it, Mr. Goolsby? and let's get going, Pap, and such things —trying to ignore the state of my shoes and trouser cuffs and the grains of dirt I could feel through my socks. But he seemed oblivious of me, watching her with his mouth half open on his worn-off teeth as if counting the soap-bubble notes spreading up into the moss. I was making up my mind to tell her to put the thing away, maybe the damn thing, when he unfolded his arms and spit in his right hand, and I was glad I didn't have to stop her; the ordered sounds made a sunlight in the place.

We dug, the old man and I, meeting in the middle, digging back each to his end, shaving the sides even, and she went on playing, on and on almost continuously, paying no attention to us, moving about along the rim of trees, a singing to herself it was, one song drifting on into another, imperceptibly to my ear though after a time I would realize that something had changed a little; sometimes she went back through a piece, moving it up or down, not much tune to a lot of it but a planned progression always, long swift chains of sound leading into sustaining notes that you could fore-hear though you didn't know just what way you were going to reach them, the sustaining notes themselves in a progression to each other. Sometimes you lost sight of her altogether, the sounds coming back from it was hard to say where, almost out of the hanks of moss, then she would appear again, maybe farther upstream, or down, and the notes would all return familiarly to her, swarming, large and small, about her head. Once, leaning on the spade catching my breath, I watched her draw a long note from end to end of the bow, pulling it out with a slow steady care that reminded me of seaside bridges and the careful hauling up of a loose-hung crab. She stopped, having netted him, and brushed a twist of hair off her forehead with the back of her hand; she smiled at me across the grayed grass, her mouth open anyway I guess. "Bach always manages a happy landing," she said, and took off again, biting her lower lip, the color up in her cheeks.

There was something in the music I had never heard before, not consciously. I suppose the water, the woods, the quantities of draping moss had some effect on the actual sound but what I heard was beyond the sound itself, something the sound drew along with it, and I thought I knew there bending over the miserable ditch what it was she sought in "breaking out the fiddle." She had said courage, but I thought it was not courage exactly, not confidence. Something the opposite of disheartenment, if there is such a word; enheartenment, maybe. Something, radarlike, scanning for light through what the Cardinal called encircling gloom. Certainly, for me, that quality was in it, and for her too, I imagine; why in it, I have no notion, unless those things—music, painting, poetry and the rest—having risen out of a deep tap into the human spirit, set up a sort of echo, a sort of harmonics, in our own deep (and forgotten) wells. A transfusion from the spirit's great bloodbank. And most of us can use a pint at any man's funeral, know him or not, for the parts of us that go with him. As Second Gravedigger at this one, up to his knees in burial, my word to her now, if she had asked me, would have been play on.

At about three feet we began to get in each other's way and Goolsby climbed out and sat on the ground with his knees up and his head hanging. He didn't seem winded; he took a couple of deep breaths and after that his bony old shoulders hardly moved.

After a few minutes he stood up and wiggled his fingers at me and I climbed out and sat on the weeds as he had done except that my muscles, all of them, felt like empty sausage skins and I couldn't get all the air I wanted even pulling it in through mouth and nose. I unwrapped the once-fresh handkerchief I had tied over my blister, broken now and the size and color of a new penny. When I got my breath back I took off my unrecognizable shoes and poured out the grit. Beyond the black pile of earth we had thrown up I could see a corner of my package sticking out from under the viola case and I was tired enough to squint straight at it and ask myself what if the thing did miss the plane? miss the magazine? How good a job was it anyhow? Honestly? Maybe the best I was capable of, but was that any answer? Asking it all, first, in a sort of luxurious what-the-hellism, feeling about for some floor to my dejection.

And coming to it right away, I thought, in the cool actuality of seeing Graham's empty desk tomorrow and hearing over all this distance what he would have to say about me and the rest of my irresponsible tribe, and getting finally to the cool question of wouldn't he simply fill in with something out of the file and put me off to the next issue? He wouldn't wash out the whole business, would he? He liked the book. He might possibly cut it another third, though, and run it in two shots instead of three. And cut the check a third too. And remember it all the next time—I can tell how tired I am by the look of my hopes. And as the edge of my tiredness dulled, the plane-missing extremity began to fade back to unacceptable and I tied my shoes and got up. "How deep do you want to go, Mr. Goolsby?"

He sat down on the rim of the grave studying the ragged spade-marks in the bottom. "You don't know how deep you dig a grave?"

"I know all right," I said, annoyed by his tone, "but I don't have all the time in the world. I've got to get my car fixed and be at the coast by four o'clock."

He said I was a long way from the coast, which had a peculiar ring, I thought, the idea striking me that if this man saw fit to break his promise I had no way of holding him to it; I could fill my part of the bargain (was filling it, in all conscience) but there was nothing to make him fill his—except, ultimately, his opinion of himself, and I didn't know what that was, Bible-carrying old fisherman-moonshiner. "You said you'd take me to a man with a car," I reminded him, seeing then the gun standing against the tree where he had leaned it and thinking there was another "except" if I waited until his back was turned, sneaked over and took possession, a possibility so remotely beyond my instincts and inclinations as to be practicallly non-existent.

He swung his tough old legs up on the surface. "If I said I would I will."

I mumbled some sort of thanks, wondering if there was a hedge in this way of putting it, and lowered myself again between the soft sides.

I had dug only a few spadefuls when, toward the river end, I lifted out a clod that had a gleam on the under side, then lifted out another, then stood there looking at the gleam where the clods had come from. I beckoned to him, trying to disguise the way I felt; I would rather have seen that gleam than gold. I said, "We're about to hit water," and he gave a reluctant nod.

I smoothed the shovel-marks out of the bottom, tramped it down, while he pulled some moss and scattered it in the coffin, then we laid the body on it, nailed the lid and with two pieces of rope looped under the ends, the old man and the girl and I lowered the sheeted length of Jared Goolsby into the ground. It is an impressive act, for all its simplicity and everydayness, for all our crust of hedonism—which most of us keep intact by not putting too much weight on it; we may turn away with a shrug, reaching out for the trusty bottle, but we have seen, the surface of us has and the depths too, somehow. I looked down on the end of this stranger who had lived about as long as I had (not so long, I had come to think), felt superior in that I was alive and inferior in that he had passed with apparently sufficient dignity a test I was yet to take, and let my eyes rise up from the knees to the bent head of the old man standing at the foot. He had jabbed the shovel into the pile of dirt between us and stood there with his hands hanging heavily down his thighs. I waited, straining my patience, for him to give some signal he was ready to fill the grave; in the silence you could hear a watery sound from the river.

When he continued to stand there I touched the handle of my spade suggestively but he didn't move for what seemed like several minutes.

Then he got the Bible and opened it to a passage that must have had associations in his memory; it seemed to have little present application except possibly the flow of the words, which as I recalled from austere readings by my father, he might have found on practically any page. It was the story of Elijah and the widow woman of Zarephath, and he read it without any glasses, unless he was reciting. It begins, "And it came to pass after these things, that the son of the woman, the mistress of the house, fell sick; and his sickness was so sore that there was no breath left in him." She appeals to Elijah, as everyone used to know though Jo was listening as if it were all new to her, and Elijah carries the boy "up into a loft, where he abode," and lays him upon his own bed and prays. "And he stretched himself upon the child three times, and cried unto the Lord, and said, O Lord my God, I pray thee, let this child's soul come into him again. And the Lord heard the voice of Elijah; and the soul of the child came into him again, and he revived. And Elijah took the child, and brought him down out of the chamber into the house, and delivered him unto his mother. And Elijah said, See, thy son liveth. And the woman said to Elijah, Now by this I know that thou art a man of God, and that the word of the Lord in thy mouth is truth."

He closed the book and I reached behind me for the spade; I was impatient to get on with it. I had slipped my watch out while he was reading and it was nearly twelve-thirty. I was getting cold too, standing there.

Then I saw he was looking at me, holding out a grimy hand as if passing me something. When he realized I didn't understand he said, "Would you kindly offer a few words in prayer?"

I didn't laugh but I came close to it, it was so unthinkable. I am not a churchman, hardly a Christian, really, in the true sense; not an "unbeliever" exactly, being unable to deny any more than to affirm on the basis of what evidence I can gather, but certainly no one to "offer a few words in prayer." If I had said a prayer since my mother's knee I couldn't remember when. It was also trying to my patience to be asked for one favor more. I shook my head. I said, "I'm afraid you'll have to excuse me—"

"Thou art a scholar; speak to it, Horatio." She said it in a monotone, in what might have been a mocking aside, looking down into the grave.

She waited and the old man waited, and I was taken back to some vague grove of cedar trees in a sandy country cemetery with a waiting cluster of bowed heads and a man in black with a white hand raised, and before I knew what I was doing I had lifted my hand, lowered my head and pronounced, after Elijah, "O Lord our God," my voice surprising me both in the sound of it and in the words.

I didn't know what to say. My only idea, now that I was into it, was to say something that would seem adequate to the old man and still not make a fool of me in the eyes of the young and brash, a practically impossible goal, I figured, and one that I might as well forget. But I was impressed to be standing there among the trees gazing down on the dead that yesterday had been the living, and I said something like here in these woods of our bewilderment we pause in respect for the great dark into which the light that once lighted this body has now returned. I said, "We *are not*, then we *are*, then we *are not*, and the why and how of it are beyond our reasoning. May the hearts be strengthened of the father and the son who remain in the light. And the hearts of the rest of us who remain too. May we go the roads that lead to understanding and compassion. May we make good use of this light that burns in us for a while."

I meant this as the end, but the old man stood there with his heavy hands, not seeming to realize I had finished, and I remembered something I had heard once in the pueblos of New Mexico and I said, "May our roads come in safely; may our roads all be fulfilled. May it not somehow become difficult for us when we have gone but a little way. May we grow old. May our roads reach all the way to Dawn Lake. May our roads be fulfilled."

"Amen," he said; he seemed satisfied. He leaned over and picked up a handful of earth, said, "The Lord has given, the Lord has took away," and tossed it onto the lid. He turned his eyes toward Jo's feet. "The fiddle, ma'am?" with a question mark, motioning toward the open case and the instrument propped in it.

She went to it without a word, took it up, brushed her thumb across a chord with a swift delicacy and while we filled the grave played something on the lower strings that laid over the whole uncouth clearing a kind of serene prestige, the sound-lineage leading back through centuries to gray cathedrals far removed from our forest and river but linked to us by the sounds, the same sounds. And the same occasion.—It was quite a burial and I sometimes wonder what sort of man it was we buried, sometimes think we buried more there than Jared.

When we had shaped the earth into a decent mound we gathered up the implements, the old man and I, and took them down to the boat; she followed us, the viola wrapped and put away, my box and coat bundled with the other case under her arm. I washed my hands and forearms in the river, the water searing my blisters like iodine. The damp air chilled you as soon as you stopped moving and I was glad to roll down my sleeves and get into my coat. As we stood there while Goolsby stowed the gear then picked his way over the seats into the stern she put out her hand and gripped mine, and I thought if the young lady is in need of support after all this I am not surprised but she has come to the wrong man; I was cold and weak and my shoulders ached and even the memory of the music couldn't wholly wipe away what I had seen. But she was giving, not asking. She approved of something, I didn't know what, and strength seemed to pour into my empty body through her fingers.

We sat together, hands locked, on one of the center thwarts that had been Jared's bier, viola, violin, manuscript, young and old; Goolsby slanted out into midstream and we picked up quite a nice speed on the current. I didn't look back; I didn't need to bring any more of it with me than was with me already. I said, "Now we can get on with it," moving my withered shirt cuff. We both looked at my watch, which said a little after one, then I looked up at the wedge of sky pointing down at the river and I knew it was no lighter gray than the sky behind but my feelings about it contradicted me; it felt lighter. I read the current into it that was with us now, the lightened boat, the easier push, read myself into it and my growing sense of release as if I had stepped back from that edge just in time. My heart was lighter, whatever the sky; for me Jared seemed to have gone off with such quantities of dark there wasn't much left. I said, "The tide has turned," not meaning it literally (I didn't think the tides reached that far up) but it was the way I felt. The mud on my shoes and trousers was beginning to dry. We were over the hill; "out of the woods" my father used to say for someone on the mend, and there in the midst of them I thought we too were out of them.

She said, "I've got some bad news for you, Wesley."

The Wesley surprised me, but there was no self-consciousness in the way she said it, maybe less than in her Mr. Johns. My inclination was to tell her I hadn't been called that since I was a child, to call me Bill, but the first-name issue always embarrasses me and I let it go, honestly rather pleased to be called that, both because her using it gave me a slightly younger complexion and because it seemed to give this unlucky day a label of its own. Besides, the "bad news" hit me as strongly as the Wesley.

I said, "Bad news?" and she leaned toward my ear with the front teeth showing and whispered, "I'm hungry."

"That's worse news for you than me," I said, my relief going into a laugh; I hadn't known what was coming.

"First I want a hitch, then I'm thirsty, now I'm hungry. I'm a mess."

I gripped her warm hand in a reassurance I knew she didn't need from the tone of her voice, but in its way it *was* bad news. It reminded me of a need of food too, though mine wasn't hunger so much as an impersonal reading on a gauge. It also reminded me that Goolsby was probably feeling the same way. I turned sideways and asked him how long he thought it would take to reach the man he had spoken of. "The man with the car." I was thinking we might get something to eat from him.

By the look on his face I believed for a minute he was going to pretend he didn't know what I was talking about, then he said, "I've got to eat me some dinner first thing I do."

The idea of another stop was exasperating just to think of and I said, "Can't this man with the car give us something to eat after we get there?"

He hardly bothered to shake his head, a slight wag, looking off down the river over our heads, and I returned to the "man with the car," asking again how long it would take; I let him see me glancing at my watch, wanting him to know I had time on my mind. "Half an hour? Hour? Two hours?" He admitted almost reluctantly it wouldn't take two and I said, "One?"

"Might do it in one on a going tide."

I said I'd like to get there by two-thirty.

His only answer was to pat his concave stomach and I wondered if he didn't enjoy being tantalizing. It was either that, I thought, which was harmless enough, or else he had no intention of taking us and wasn't yet ready to say so, which I didn't really believe. We had filled our part of the agreement in good faith; there was no reason to suppose he would do any less.

In either case I didn't see what I could do at the moment. If it was his idea to stop at the house and get some food there was time enough for that (my "two-thirty" had been stretching it a little toward the safe side), and the more we talked about food the less inclined I was to wait an hour also. But at five or ten minutes to two we ought to be shoving off; before that if possible but not any later. If we weren't, then it would be time to do something—what, I couldn't quite foresee, with no cards left, but something. The whole day seemed to be unrolling without the help of any cards of mine, which might have given it an unreal aspect except that I could remember many an actual misfortune or break of luck materializing without my willing it; I didn't have to go beyond my blisters to know if it was real.

He said, as if to himself more than to either of us, "Hervin must have found Luke Mole," which made no sense to me until I noticed a thin blue ribbon of smoke trailing out low over the water from beyond a bend, trailing out with a sort of mockery at me and my discomforts, at all I had been forced to undergo, none of it necessary if we had waited a few minutes longer. But my first anger faded away; maybe I should have been poorer without it. When we came into the clear I saw the white mule standing at a corner of the porch.

# FOUR

As I stepped over the bow to the bank the Indian appeared from somewhere and dragged the flat bottom a few feet up on the land, taking no more notice of me than if he had never seen me before; he wrapped the rusty bow chain round a tree trunk the way he would probably tether the mule. I think Hervin had seen us out on the river and gone to his menagerie because he came from behind the house now with a raccoon in his arms on a wire and stood there looking at Jo to catch her eye. The Indian said, "Where's Jared, Mr. Boyce? Hervin said you wanted me and I thought Jared must be sick but he ain't here."

Goolsby stood up in the boat as if he had heard nothing. He threw the shovels out on the bank and reached back for the ax and the gun. Then he said coldly, "You see them shovels, don't you?"

The Indian picked up the implements, his manner changing. "I'm mighty sorry, Mr. Boyce. I thought Jared would be with us for a long time." I thought he might have been doctor enough to know what Jared's condition had been, guessed the rest from what Hervin had told him; anyhow he wasn't surprised, made no pretense of being.

The old man said, "Who's that in there? Sarah?" and Mole said, "When I thought Jared was sick I went by home and brought Sarah to help. I told her to get a shad out of the pen. I thought you'd be along pretty soon. Mr. Boyce, if you'd got hold of me last night I might could have give him something."

Goolsby said never mind.

I didn't know what it was all about and cared less. All that mattered to me was that nothing between them developed into any cause to delay us. And there seemed to be no reason it should; they walked off together and the Indian put the shovels under the porch as if he knew where they belonged, held out his hand for the ax and stood it beside the base of the chimney. Goolsby propped the gun against the steps, a reassuring little detail to me, taking it as acknowledgment we would be going on shortly.

On the porch a tall young woman, maybe thirty, maybe thirty-five, came out of the door wiping her hands on a homemade apron and embraced him. I thought she might be a daughter, then I knew she wasn't; her skin had a flat almost gold color that I thought meant some sort of cross, part Indian or part Oriental, part Negro maybe. She had evidently been weeping and she wept again as the old man put his arm round her, turning off abruptly and going back inside. She was quite handsome, none of the usual stoop.

I laid the manuscript on the steps by the gun—symbols in my mind of our continuing journey—poured some water out of a bucket I saw into a tin basin, washed with a yellow scrap of soap, dashed the water over the yard with the feeling of pulling a chapter-end out of a typewriter, the smell of frying fish and coffee floating a peculiar sunniness on the damp air that I said to myself spitefully was as sunny as anything Bach had floated; I felt things were better than I had been supposing. Jo went in the house with the boy as I was cleaning my shoes on what was left of my hand-kerchief; it wasn't much of a job, the Indian sitting on his heel against a bay tree watching me past an end of the long table with the bottles and jars. When I finished I walked toward him, saying something about Hervin finding him; it sounded much too chitchat in that environment but you get used to saying something when you approach some-body. Dr. Mole's answer was to pick up a twig, finger it, snap off a piece and flip it away with his thumb.

He said, "That paper you wrote on," stopping as if it were a question.

It took me a few seconds to know what he was talking about, my thoughts stumbling to the manuscript paper I had written so much on, then I nodded and he said, "I give it to a man in a car going to Rucker."

"You did!" I said, everything changing. "Why didn't you tell me?"

"I'm telling you."

"Did he say he'd phone from Rucker?"

"We looked under the hood, how you didn't have any belt. He said there might be a belt in Rucker."

It was disheartening to see how my wrong decision had grown into such consequences. If I had waited I could have gone to Rucker with the man and either found a belt or talked to Cloud on the phone; I might have been on the sundeck at The West Green by now, or on one of those other beautiful, you-might-have-taken roads. I asked him whether he thought the man was going to send somebody back from Rucker if he found a belt.

"You didn't say do that."

86

"How could I tell you were going to run into a man on the way to Rucker!" It was absurd to be irritated but he seemed so offhand; I tried to amend it by thanking him for passing on my message. "Did you know the man? I mean is he somebody likely to make the call?"

He shook his head, not in a negative but indicating it was hard to say, who knows? "Ain't but one way to tell," he said.

I said, more to myself than him, getting it straight in my mind, "Cloud may be there working on it now." He said, "Chances are," and I looked about for Jo; I was tempted to change course right there, start back without waiting to eat, but when I saw her blue dress through the door, moving about the kitchen with Sarah and the boy, I thought I would wait. I was hungry too. And besides it was not a clear-cut matter. I said. "The trouble is if I go back and he's not there I'm in a worse spot then than now."

"He might get there any minute. There's nothing for you in here."

I looked at him because it was just filtering through to me he might be wanting me to go back, at any rate to leave them and that was the promptest way; but his smooth hairless face told me nothing. I said the old man was taking me down the river as soon as we got something to eat. "He says there's somebody down there with a car."

He said in a conspiratorial tone, "Mr. Boyce ain't what he used to be. You can't always go by what he says," and I said, "You mean there's nobody a little way down with a car? About an hour down?"

"You might have to go all the way to Bluffton to get a car."

"But Bluffton's at the coast, isn't it?"

"Near about. On the Sound. Three or four hours getting to Bluffton."

He made getting there such an unattractive prospect I wondered if he planned it that way. I could believe Goolsby had misled me, needing my help; I could also believe this man was misleading me now or trying to. It was hard to choose between them. And hard to say where this one's misleading might begin; maybe he hadn't seen anybody going to Rucker at all. I gazed at the pink malignant coils in one of the jars, only half seeing them; I was about to say I would ask Goolsby whom he had in mind, when the Indian said, watching me, "This must be new territory for you, Mister."

I said I didn't know it too well. I couldn't tell whether he was getting at anything or not but I remembered the attitude Goolsby had taken at first and the boy and my impulse was to bring it out in the open by saying in so many words if he thought I was a cop he was wrong and could forget it. Then I caught myself; after all it might be helpful to leave that possibility in his head if it was there. I didn't know what sort of people they were. They probably had a still or two around there somewhere and would be happier to see the last of a revenue man than a mere book writer, a parting I was certainly in favor of speeding. I told him I had done some fishing along the coast and let it go at that, mumbling something about "dinner" (as I knew they called it) and turning away toward the house.

He threw away the stick and stood up in the paratrooper boots, brushing his hands. He asked if we had taken Jared to the island, as if dismissing the subject, but I hardly heard him for wondering again which of these two to believe. Neither one promised anything for sure. If I went back to the highway the car might not be fixed and there I'd be, but at three o'clock instead of ten; if I went with Goolsby there might be no help that way either. I said, "Yes, we buried Jared on the island."

He picked up one of the jars and shook the alcohol and said idly, "You notice anything about Jared?" When I asked him what he meant he didn't answer for a minute then he said, "Him and the old man never got along."

I chose to see no implication in it; their feuds didn't concern me, whether it was one between father and son or, which I thought was more likely in the light of this gratuitous suggestion, one between the old man and Luke. I wasn't interested in anything but getting on my way— whichever way it was to be. And if there was any kind of undercover tension among these people I was more interested in getting on my way than ever; I could imagine some low-burning quarrel between them flaring up and delaying us, maybe even changing Goolsby's mind about taking us. I shrugged and turned toward the house, wondering if I couldn't push things along; before I reached the steps Jo was beckoning from the door.

The table top was damp from a recent scrubbing— Sarah's, no doubt—and we sat down country style leaving the chairs toward the stove for the women. The old man bowed his head and said a blessing, brief and perfunctory but with a respect for the non-animal in us that I respected, and we ate the brown squares of hot fish and the darker brown squares of cornbread and drank the coffee, all of it good to my taste. And evidently to Jo's too, though neither of us had a way with fish-bones comparable to Goolsby's and the Indian's or even the boy's, all of them forking up the fish, bones and all, then pulling out the bones, mouths like pincushions—an unlovely sight but I cared little.

Sarah didn't sit down, and when Goolsby said to her,

"Get me that honey over there, Sarah, ma'am. I don't take to sorghum. There in the cupboard," adding aloud but as if to himself, "Jared was the man for sorghum," she turned her face to the wall and clutched the apron in a ball against her mouth. It only lasted a few seconds and you heard nothing to indicate sobbing but when she brought the dish of honey her eyes in their dark sockets were wet and pink. I saw Luke watching her over a piece of half-eaten cornbread, jaws not moving, putting the cornbread slowly down, and I thought this man is going to jump up and slap his wife across the face. Maybe she thought so too for she moved away at once, back to the stove; he looked after her, jaws beginning to chew again, and in a minute picked up the cornbread.

There was one thing I had to get straight before I could begin to decide which direction to take, back by land or on by water, and I said, "Mr. Goolsby, Luke thinks the nearest car would be at Bluffton. That's a long way." Neither one of them said anything, Luke not hearing maybe, still thinking of Sarah, the old man silently pulling great pinches of white bones from his lips. When his tongue was free he mumbled as he cut into the fish, "Three or four cars at the plantation. Plenty cars."

Luke said, "Better not take him to the plantation, Mr. Boyce."

Goolsby said impatiently, "I'll let him out half a mile this side," and Luke accepted it, or seemed to, glancing at me and bringing up again the matter of my car being perhaps already fixed, which I hadn't wanted to mention to the old man, fearing he might use it as a pretext for not making the river trip; the question was which way were my chances best? and I didn't want to listen to arguments and suggestions put out on some other basis. Luke told about the man going to Rucker, it was two men now in a '48 Chevrolet.

Goolsby asked him who it was but he said he had never seen them before. "Talk like coast people."

Hearing it again it sounded possible; one man or two men, that didn't invalidate it. I believed it. Which really reduced the matter to the driver of the Chevrolet; if he gave Cloud the message I was satisfied Cloud would come, or send one of the boys. There might have been some trouble in getting Cloud to take a collect call, unless the driver had got a chance of saying it was from me; if Cloud refused it, would the man have spent thirty or forty cents to put it through? He might have or he might not; you couldn't tell without knowing the man. I thought there was a fair chance he would have got the call through somehow. And even if he hadn't there was the other chance that he might have sent somebody back with a belt from Rucker. Considering all that against the background of my not liking the idea of the river trip anyhow, for the time it would take, for the uncertainty of where we were headed, and for other reasons I wasn't too clear about (if they were reasons), I listened to the story leniently—and wondered how Jo was listening, studying Luke across her coffee cup with the same steady cool appraisal she had given me and probably all the rest of her pick-ups. She glanced at me once, maybe to see how I was taking it. When he had finished, ending up by repeating that my car might be sitting there ready to go by this time, she looked down into the coffee cup and said, "That's retracing your steps."

I didn't care what you called it, if the car was fixed it would save us hours. And if we got back there, it occurred to me now, and the car was not fixed, somebody else might come along; the Chevrolet proved there were people passing now and then. And the prospect of getting out of the shade and gloom of this inner region was almost irresistible, though I knew that was an irrelevant consideration.

She said, "It's usually better not to back up," recalling the woods to me and her scorn of the cal-cu-lated risk. It irritated me now as it had then and I said, "Sometimes it's the only possible way to save your neck."

She didn't answer, gazing down into the cup with her teeth showing.

But it was enough to get me off the fence and I told him we would go by the river. It was a long walk back; I was tired; I think there was also in my mind an irrational idea that her impulses were better than mine. His plate was empty, clean practically, and I set down my half-drunk coffee and said, "What about shoving off?"

He laid his skinny fingers on the edge of the table in a sort of response, but before he could say anything Luke said, "Let me see you a minute, Mr. Boyce," and Goolsby said, "Wait for me outside." I supposed it was about signing the death certificate, but anyhow there was nothing to do but go and I beckoned to Jo with my head and went out on the porch. I didn't know what was going on under the surface here, or if anything was; I didn't want to know. It was a little like trying to relax the muscles of your forehead and scalp, denying a headache. My watch showed three or four minutes to two. If he came on now we were doing all right. No time to throw away but enough.

I picked up the manuscript and the fiddle cases and walked across the yard to the water and set them in the boat. I figured Goolsby would be taking his gun and I went back to it, propped against the side of the steps where he had left it. Jo came out of the house as I was lifting it, a cheap gun, no carving, nothing fancy but somehow seeming a part of the old man like a pair of his shoes or his faded hat, the wooden parts a deep brown from the oil of his hands—and of "papa's" too in all probability, a family gun. I unbreeched it, out of habit, not thinking, and then stood there looking at the brass disc in each barrel as she hopped down the steps, feeling as if I had opened somebody else's mail. I suppose I had been thinking it might be loaded, could be, but this proof was a shock to me just the same. I breeched it ("britched" it was more appropriate), checked the safety and set it back against the steps. She could have seen the shells but I didn't think she had. I said, "What's keeping him?"

Parts of two front teeth were visible but they didn't suggest a smile. "They're talking about who goes," she said. "Luke says he'll take us."

"Luke?" I had been afraid nobody would take us and now we had competition.

"He says he wants to get some stuff in the town, sugar and grits, he says."

I couldn't see that it mattered much who took us, as long as whoever it was knew where to put us ashore; I said well, okay, it made no difference to us. She glanced down at the buttons of the long overcoat, which she had put on again, the air off the river quite sharp now. She said, "I'd rather it was the old man."

I might have preferred the old man too; I found them both unpleasant, in different ways but to much the same degree, except that I thought I did perceive some of the things the old man valued, which gives you a basis for dealing with a person. When you don't know what a man values you don't know how to appeal to him. But I said to cheer her up I didn't see there was much to choose between them. She said, "Can't you tell the old man the bargain was he would take us?"

I said, "I don't care who takes us as long as we get going." Her dejection reminded me of her fiddles and I told her I had put them in the boat. She looked me in the eye for a second and led the way toward the bank; out of earshot, gazing at the river, she said, "Something's the matter in there."

I asked her what she was talking about and she said she didn't know. "But something's the matter. You can feel it. That woman, Sarah, she's not just grieving, she's heartbroken." I took her hand; I wouldn't have presumed to but she had begun it and I remembered the peculiar strength that can pass through the touch of people's hands. Her fingers were cold. "I'd lay a fiddle on it she was Jared's girl."

This opened up far too many contingencies and I fell back on a chilly detachment that has often come in handy and smiled at her imaginings; I said maybe so, maybe not, those things were no concern of ours. "Our concern is simple: get out of here as quickly as possible." There is no end to the tangle you can get into meddling in other people's business, or the tangle you usually get the business into. "Of course," I said, "we could skip all this by going back to the car."

She pulled her hand away in some irritation. "You're always trying to 'go back,' Wesley. You can't retract. You've got to burn the bridge." I pointed out that the car might just possibly be fixed but she didn't register. "You've got to go the full circle."

I said, "That means going in the boat. Probably with Luke."

"All right then, we go in the boat. With Luke."

I was really glad to have it put securely into words. I thought now if, when I got to the car with help, I should find it had already been repaired I wouldn't even feel bad about it. You can't expect to decide today's question on tomorrow's information. I said, "Suits me."

I went up on the porch and stood in the open door. They were sitting there at the table, the papers between them, and the stub of a pencil. Sarah was doing something over at the stove; the boy had gone. I spoke to the old man, as if assuming he would be the one to take us, recognizing in my mind now the thought that it was still possible neither one of them was going to take us. I told him firmly I had to go now. "We struck a bargain, you know, Mr. Goolsby."

For answer he put the papers in the envelope and pushed it at Luke. I think I have never had an answer I wanted more. Luke said to Sarah, "Let's have the lantern." He stuffed the envelope in the musette bag and walked out, lantern, bag, coat, pistol belt and a can of what I supposed was gasoline.

I laid two ten-dollar bills on the table. "I want to pay for using the boat," I said, but he was pushing the money back to me before I finished saying it. He said, "The kingdom of heaven is within you, and whoever shall know himself shall find it. You'll need your hat. It'll be cold on the river."

"I didn't bring a hat," I said. "You see, I didn't expect—"

"Give him his hat, Sarah. Right there on the nail."

"It's Jared's hat, Mr. Boyce."

"Give him his hat."

She handed me a black wool hat, the kind they wear in that country, and I took it; it seemed the simplest thing to do. I thought his grief had been more upsetting to him than I realized; I was sure of it when, shaking my hand, he ꞁulled me down where he was sitting and, instead of saying

95

something in my ear, which I was ready for, kissed me greasily on the cheek. In my Anglo-Saxon confusion I turned to Sarah for an understanding look but she had gone.

I went down the steps with the hat in my hand (I somehow flinched from putting it on though it must have been Jared's Sunday hat—or rather, Saturday night—not much worn, the crown in a dome), beckoned impatiently to Jo at the trestle table with the boy and hurried to the boat and the Indian unwinding the chain from the tree.

# FIVE

From the middle of the river I glanced back. Hervin was standing with Sarah in the yard, among the trees, not on the bank; I didn't see the old man. The putty-white mule seemed hardly to have moved an ear while we had been there. Then the branches and moss and trunks worked in between us and it was all behind me. We were on the center seat, complete with manuscript and all fiddles, and I said with a sigh up from all my depths, "Well, we made it!" which seemed fair to say; allowing an hour we should be there about three. I showed her the ten-after-two on my watch but she didn't look, gazing down the water with no expression at all and undoing a middle button of the great khaki coat and letting me see the barrel of the old man's gun; the stock protruded an inch or two at the bottom but I didn't think it would be visible to Luke in the stern, what with the folds of the coat behind her heels and the almost solid thwart the seat rested on. She mumbled, biting her lip, "If the doctor can pack a gun I don't see why we can't."

The first thought I could get into words was that the damned thing was loaded and she eased her hand into a big side pocket and without looking down slipped out the two shells for a second and put them back. I said, "All right," but I didn't much like it; these kids see too many movies.

She said, "I just borrowed it. The way you borrowed the hat."

She told me I had better put it on and I gathered myself together and did, denting the crown to make it mine. It fitted. That is, it was the right size; it didn't feel right. She smiled at the effect. "It belonged to the old man?" I side-stepped admitting I had on a dead man's hat by saying yes; I argued it really was the old man's now with Jared gone, but I was sorry I had said it, sitting there in the wind wondering in a flash of sadness if I hadn't been sidestepping one thing or another all my life, compromising, bending, escape hatch always more or less ajar, behind me always at least one unburned bridge. I said, "Might have been Jared's," and felt a little better.

I was glad to have it anyhow. The air was colder than in the morning; maybe the wind had changed or we had swung more into it, or maybe the tide did reach up that high and was running out and we were making more speed. It seemed to me there was a sea smell in the air but I thought that was hardly possible. We must have been a long way from the coast, though certainly a good deal closer to the Sound and the salt creeks and estuaries that I remembered fingered up innumerably into that land, making it as hard to separate ocean and continent as night and day. Now and then we would pass through a band of river smell, thick and fish-heavy and coated with the moldy scent of rotting wood and freshwater mud, then on into the sea smell again, or a suggestion of it that seemed not to be there if you sucked it in and tried to catch it—which I did again and again, trying to fasten on something that was to me so clean and beneficent, so un-baleful. My mother used to say the Indians took all their illnesses to the sea, and I remembered how I used to feel that if I could reach the sea I should somehow be complete. The daylight had toppled over subtly on to the down slope; already I thought you could sense here and there a layer of evening gathering over the water, a sort of pre-mist. I wasn't surprised when she shuddered and said, "I'm cold."

I said, teasing her but with a trace of bitterness too, cataloguing, "Well, you were thirsty. And then after a while you were hungry. And now you're cold."

"I'll bet you're sorry as hell you gave me a hitch," the great shoulders of the coat shaking at the joke she had played on me, the bill of goods she had sold me, yet I thought a little wistful too, sorry at my being sorry. I let it rest for a moment then I said deliberately, "The simple fact of the matter is I am *not* sorry," and I was surprised to see her lower her eyes to her lap as if I had told her she was beautiful; I wondered if her self-confidence went as deep as I had been thinking. She said, "I'm a lot of trouble to you," gazing ahead now, teeth showing in the enigmatic grin.

I said in a flat scientific tone, "You're more help than trouble," adding, because I meant it, "If it wasn't for you I'd have given this up long ago." I wasn't too clear as to just what I would have given up doing but I did honestly feel that if it hadn't been for her, if I had been in it alone I should by now be off on some tangent a good deal less propitious, the latest being the one leading back to the highway which I now felt would have produced nothing.

She interrupted what I was thinking by looking at me with the narrowed eyes she had once or twice turned on me in the car—though she was on the other side of me now and the eyes were minutely different—and saying, "There's something I've been wanting to ask you, Wesley," watching my expression as if to foretell what it was going to change into.

I was trying to prepare myself on as wide a range of emergency subjects as possible, thinking too that the little round ornament in the lobe of this ear was like a tiny spotlight on how she thought of herself, on the woman she knew, when she went on, "You know, I'm interested in what's in here," laying her hand on the box between us. I said with a relieved laugh that so was I, that that was what this trek was all about.

Then she said, "Suppose it doesn't make the plane," and I said, "Now wait a minute!"

She said, "Yes, I know, but just suppose."

I shook my head firmly. "I don't want to think about that." I couldn't help noticing the package was already getting travel worn, a corner of the paper gone with my wasted message, another corner water-stained, a smudge along one side from being carried, none of it deep, however, and none of it obscuring the address.

"I know, but—it wouldn't affect what's in here."

"Look," I said. "You're a specialist in Shakespeare. This is one of those tides you take at the flood. And I don't intend to miss it."

She said with a patient smile, "I'm not trying to make you miss it, Wesley. I'm saying that no matter what happens at that end it doesn't affect what's in here."

It seemed pretty other-world to me, pretty far removed from sin and shame; and pretty far removed from what I had been led to expect of her generation. In any case it irked me to have success dismissed so offhandedly. "If you're saying I can get it published whether it runs in the magazine or not—"

"I'm not saying that."

"Or even that twenty-four hours' delay won't throw it out of the magazine—"

"What I'm saying, Wesley, is that the book's in here." The diamond smile was earnest but I found it unappealing. I said, "You're too far uptown for me. I'm a professional writer. I'm an old pro at this game." (I try not to use the expression very much but I always like the way it makes me feel and it slipped out.)

She shrugged her shoulders and turned her head away to the woods on the other bank, bare and tangled and gray like an old brushpile. I would have lighted a cigarette as punctuation but it was impossible in the wind; I had tried. In a minute she switched her eyes to the wilderness on my bank, hesitated a second and then said with the little intake of breath that was a kind of laugh, "You know, Wesley, I think you've been misleading yourself."

I said, "Hunh?" and she elaborated. "I think you've been mixing yourself up with somebody else."

I said to myself I had given this kid too much leeway, what with the circumstances and all; now she was going to be pleased to tell "Wesley" how to run his business. Quite possibly his life. I said I didn't quite follow her; though I followed her well enough.

She said, as if squinting at it in the treetops, "You've blinded yourself somehow. Oedipus at Colonus. He didn't want to think about something so he put his eyes out," and I said with a coolness I had learned to use in New England, "I can assure you I have nothing in common with Oedipus at Colonus, or at Thebes."

It didn't deflect her. She said, "*All the Month of March.* That was written in your own hand."

"How can you tell on such short acquaintance what is my own hand?" I diluted the sarcasm of it with a semi-smile but there was some left. I thought she might drop the whole thing, seeing that I didn't take to it, but she went on with a certain crass determination, "It's not hard. You can tell when a man's himself. And also, the 'acquaintance' isn't so short, because I read the book. Every word.—I doubt if I'll read every word of this one."

I was more than irritated. You may not feel overjoyed if someone promises to read your new book but if someone promises you he won't it's a little hard to take. "How do you know what's in this book?" I probably said it with more exclamation than question.

"Oh I don't know the details but I have some pretty telling circumstantial evidence. I know what the editors think of it. And I think I know what you think of it."

I put out a laugh at the audacity, a snort, I suppose. "I think it's something on wheels."

"That's what you say you think."

"May I ask what I really think?"

"You are trying to misunderstand me, Wesley," watching herself draw one palm across the other in a meaningless gesture, then lifting her eyes, "but I don't think you do. I don't think it would irritate you if there wasn't something in it." I said couldn't we skip the psychoanalysis? and she said, "Here's what I mean. What have you told me about this book? What it says? What it feels? What sort of people you have made for it? What is the tone of it? Why you had to write it? Not a word. You tell me it's already a big success."

I asked her tolerantly what she had against success; that

seemed an improved attitude to take, the smile down. "I understood you were aiming at first viola in the Boston Symphony."

"Success is all right, fine thing. All the best people are successes; some a little sooner, some a little later. But when you have what the Mad Ave boys call 'instantaneous' success, that I can't put much stock in because it takes a certain amount of time to grasp something of any quality. Isn't that a characteristic of quality, that you can't appraise it at first glance? Because it's got too much."

"You're shifting now, aren't you? From success to the speed of success."

"The speed, yes. That makes you a little suspicious. And there's another thing about real success. It's got to come second, the secondary objective. The first thing is quality. If you make success the first thing you're more than likely to skimp the quality.—But you've got me off the track. Maybe that's what you meant to do," the clean eyes narrowed in a smile that was also a search.

I thought that may have been in the back of my head too so I pretended not to know what she was driving at. I hoped she would leave it alone; I wasn't in much of a mood for generalities. I didn't feel in much of a place for generalities. But "hitching" had possibly taught her patience and perseverance—if one driver passes you by, thumb another —and after a minute or two she said, "I wasn't thinking about Success, big S, but about this success," nudging the box with her elbow in a way that tried me to such a point that I said, "Listen. You have no basis for questioning the quality of this book. I didn't tell you more about it because I have found most people are not interested. And also because I've found if you talk about a book you don't write it."

"But this one's already written."

I said, "It's an old habit," probably with enough asperity to affect her for she said, "I just wanted to be sure it was written in your own hand."

"Can you write in anybody else's?"

"Oh, easily. It's very difficult to write in your own hand, to do anything in your own particular way, eliminating borrowings, thefts and dodges of various kinds. Or assimilating them. And outwitting the U.S. censors."

"The who?"

"We have a sort of capitalistic censorship, quite comparable to what Communist writers are up against. The FBI doesn't force you to write for money but public opinion just about does, by placing you as a considerable fool if you don't. Materialism is our Party Line and you'd better hold to it or pack up for Outer Mongolia."

I was about to grumble something but she went on, "There are not many honors in our country, mostly rewards. I figure the only thing you've got to offer in this world is your own point of view. It may not be worth a damn but you've got to stand or fall with it.—I'm an artist. It may sound like boasting to say so but it's really pride. I believe art is the end product, or at least as far as we can consciously go. Things turn round and round, love and birth and death, getting nowhere, until, all of a sudden, bang! here's Beethoven. That makes a difference. That's what it was all about. That does it. You don't improve on that; you move on down to another corner. People have babies and the babies have babies, and on and on until, all of a sudden, here's, well Cézanne, maybe. And that makes a difference. But in the meantime, while things are building up steam enough there are lots of us little artists. You might say we don't amount to anything but the reason I get such a kick out of being one of them is that the fundamental thing we stand for is quality. You can't have a shoddy work of art. If it's art, it's quality. And that's why art is so important, it's the breeding ground of quality. Of imagination and perceptiveness and daring too, but principally, I think, of quality."

I said, "There's such a thing as science, you know," but it didn't bother her for more than a couple of seconds.

"The trouble with science is it's just interested in truth."

"Just truth."

"You can't find truth because truth is always changing. It never stays the same two centuries running, two decades nowadays. Can you imagine Galileo addressing the Institute for Advanced Study, or Newton either? A few might go out of politeness, if they are polite. But if Mozart appeared at Juilliard you'd have to call out the National Guard. And even with the temporary truths, some are benign but a great many are malignant. Art is interested in something quite different, not truth but enlightenment, illumination. Something that's going to last a while, that we're all instinctively proud of, something that will show tomorrow's people what we were inside."

"Do you think that matters?"

"Well, it gives you a pretty good reason for wanting to look your best inside.—If it sounds corny that's just because of the way I put it. I'm not a poet."

It was pretty overwhelming. And even granting she would see the truth (or rather, see it all differently) in a few years I couldn't help being impressed. I said, "You know, Josephine, I think you are quite somebody."

She glanced at me as if to see whether I was joking then amazed me by slowly turning crimson and, after briefly fighting it, ducking her face into her hands. "I do this at the drop of a hat. Isn't it disgusting! I don't know what's the matter with me. No doubt the shrinkers would have a nasty explanation. Psychiatry is just the search for the lowest common motivation. I'm only trying to cover up, you see. Anyway, I'm not so cold now. And I'm not so unusual, really. Why do you think I am?"

I could have given her a number of reasons, even the one that it required an unusual person to take so much of the satisfaction out of my achievement, but the last one I had noticed was still prominent in my mind and I said, "People nowadays aren't concerned with quality. Equality, yes; by all means. But not quality. You believe in quality." I told her I got the feeling, from the books and plays and poetry of young people, that they practically made a cult of shoddiness. "Shoddy language, shoddy clothes, shoddy ethics, shoddy citizenship." She said, "Feeling round for something fresh, untried," and I said it seemed to me the most untried thing they could try would be quality. She said, "They're trying for a new sort of quality," paused and held me under her two blue electric spotlights until I began to see the corner I had worked myself into; I could feel a flush of my own crawling up behind my ears even before she laid her hand on my package.

But she didn't get to say it.

I hadn't seen the trestle emerging from beyond the screen of a point, and the huge growling hoot that rose out of the woods snapped me up into a moment of ancient terror, my mind jumping back a million years to brontosaur and paleoscincus as if completely sure that was what their bellow had sounded like. It startled her too, and the next thing I heard was the hollow thump of the gun butt against the bottom as the barrel slid down the inside of her coat.

The Indian seemed to be waiting for the three additional

grunts of the horn, for as the last one rattled away between the tree walls he said, "I'll take the gun, ma'am. Just sit where you are, and you too, Mister, and pass it right back behind you."

I couldn't see whether he had pulled the pistol or not but he had it and he might have. I muttered, "Give it to him," and she did; there was nothing else to do. She handed it back with an innocence that was almost amusing, as if he had suggested an idea she approved of, keeping it out of the damp or relieving her of the trouble of carrying it.

Above the motor-sounds I heard him unbreech it and snap it closed and I sat there waiting for him to demand the shells and thinking if he did I would take them and somehow get them over the side unseen; losing the gun was bad enough without loading it for him. But he didn't ask for them and we went on steadily toward the middle span, the importance of it seeming to grow less. I told myself I couldn't have pointed the gun at anybody, certainly not have pulled the trigger, any more than I could have stood up and conducted Jo's Boston Symphony; it wasn't in my line. Or in hers either. And unless you are capable of using something like that it is merely provocation to the other man; you're at his mercy anyway and it may be an honester mercy if he is quiet than if he is excited. It would have been a little better if we hadn't had the gun to lose but the next best thing, I argued, was to have it no longer.

Then watching the trestle and the striped nose of the diesel grinding out of the forest I began to see that this man didn't know my incapacities the way I did; if I had had the gun he couldn't have been sure I might not use it. It would have been a deterrent of sorts; now we had nothing—a young woman and a man with a hundred and fifty dollars in his pocket in a region that seemed all the more remote for the markets and schedules and throngs implicit in the locomotive and the engineer idly watching us through the girder-cage from under his puffed-up cap and beginning to rock his gauntlet in the traditional hail and farewell of my boyhood. You always prepare for the wrong perils (except now and then, when you have decided they are the wrong ones, you will get a double surprise by being right after all), but I could imagine extremities now in which I could pull a trigger, having one to pull.

Jo waved with a Miss Rheingold insouciance, and I waved because I couldn't think of any signal that would transmit the lack of insouciance I felt, telling myself at the same time we were not threatened in any way. What difference did it make if we knew nothing about this man except that he was evidently some sort of quack, went around armed and possibly looked on me as the law? Maybe it implied a sense of guilt, but not necessarily guilt of anything more than a little moonshining. He wanted us out, that was clear enough, but no more than we wanted to get out; our interests were not opposed. Even if he wanted us out so badly as to see to it himself, not leave it to the old man, that still created no opposition in me; it didn't matter to me who got us out.

And yet I somehow wanted to make the engineer remember he had seen us. To what end I couldn't say, perhaps just to have him take that much of us on board his invulnerable transport and out again to the everyday—the same, I suppose, as our useless whistles and signals at the blimp; a throw us a line, you that are saved. But I could think of nothing that would mark us; would have marked us, because he was across now, goggles lingering on us indulgently, not to let go too quickly of a welcome diversion from the wilderness behind and ahead but shoving up the speed, the trestle banging under the chain of earth-colored crates marked with sunny stencils from far-off sanctuaries —*Santa Fe All the Way, Union Pacific, Route of the Hiawathas, The Texas Chief, The Line of Mid-America*— then an interlude of trussed-up flats and then, as we floated closer, our motor-sounds wiped clean away in the roar, a trestleful of yellow discs trailing the sticky smell of pine and resin over the water to us like a rope just out of reach, all of it solid, assured, the self-confident thunder seeming to block the spans.

It felt as if we were steering straight at a wall, the current sweeping us at the black piles of the breakwaters then between them into a raceway between the piers, the tumult towering up in front of us as though, for a blow, then straight into the roots of blinding sound that was like being tripped and tumbled in an onslaught of breakers. Then, after one of those indeterminate lengths of time, long or longer, out again into a steadying world that seemed to be a continuation of the old but that you felt must be different and different forever, her head buried, hands over ears, in my lap, my chest against her shoulders, shielding, cringing myself, I don't know.

She lifted up slowly as the din subsided and flung at him, "Why didn't you wait till it passed!" dropping her voice to a whispered you bastard, for the pain he had put us through.

The Indian said, "Chute the chutes," with a grin in his tone and I said something silly about time and tide, hoping to pass it all off before he got mad, which we couldn't afford. She saw the manuscript box in an inch of bilgewater in the bottom and retrieved it, wiping it on the skirt of her coat. I took it, dried it after a fashion with my damp handkerchief and told her it wasn't hurt. The horn came back out of the swamp in a faraway gentle hum and I looked round at the caboose entering the cage, the motor-sounds rising up again as if from a deep dive. I managed a placating smile for him; no harm had been done. We were still afloat and on our way—though perhaps a slightly new way; I wondered, from her having leaned against me and made me glance for a second at the question I had asked myself way back in pre-fanbelt days about how to get rid of her, reaching Waltonville; made me see I would now be getting rid of an entirely different her.

I asked him how much farther it was and he said, "Where to?"

"To the man with the car, of course, the plantation or wherever he is."

He gazed off at the moss-draped banks as if he hadn't heard me and I was about to ask him again when he said, "Much better for you to go on to town." I said, "Town!" and he said, "Bluffton's a going town. No trouble finding a car in Bluffton."

I didn't like the sound of it and I said, "The old man said there was somebody with a car along in here."

He spit over the motor into the foam, much as the old man himself had done. "Mr. Boyce ain't been down here in twenty years."

I said, "You mean there's nobody in here with a car?" I could hardly put it into words.

"If they got a car at the plantation they wouldn't let you have it. Just a bunch of rich Yankees come down here shooting up all the game. I know 'em. Guided for 'em one season."

"You just drop us off there. I'll take a chance on the car." It was the best news I had heard all day. You don't buy up a plantation without all sorts of cars; they might spare me not only a car but a belt and somebody who knew how to put it on. I had been trying not to look at the time any more often than I could help, not to torture myself, but I looked now. It was three twenty-seven exactly. If my car was ready to go in an hour and a half I could make it, and without running too many speed traps either. "Did you hear that?" I said to her.

I thought she hadn't because she showed none of my elation but she said, without taking her eyes from the squared bow, voice smothered under the motor-sounds, "He wants to take us to Bluffton." I said I didn't care what he wanted, this was where we got off. "Bluffton must be twenty miles from here."

She shook her head with a doleful smile. "I don't know. But we do what he says." I knew she was thinking of the gun but I didn't agree with her; we had no weapons but I had some money. I thought I had paid enough already (one way and another, more than I had ever paid for anything) but if I had to I would pay again. "Why should he want to take us to Bluffton?"

She moved the great shoulders of the coat, said you tell me, then, "Maybe these people have got something on him. Maybe he thinks they would report him to the cops. You're a cop, you know."

"I don't believe he takes me for a cop. And anyway, if they were going to turn him in for something they could have done it before this. They didn't have to wait for Special Officer Johns."

She studied my face for a minute then turned back to the river, then to the bottom of the boat. I could hardly hear her voice, but I did hear it and it said, "You're satisfied, Wesley, that was a natural death?"

It surprised me and I said, "What death?" as if trying to tell myself I had forgotten. She said Jared and I said of course I was satisfied, why not? "You don't have to live in New York to have a heart attack."

She said in her monotone to the boat-bottom, "I think the gentleman in the back row is a killer."

"Oh, Jo!"

She asked me if I had taken a good look at Sarah and I said not specially. I hadn't paid much attention. She said, "Sarah knows he did it. And knows why."

I remembered she had been in the kitchen with Sarah and I said, "Did she tell you something?" She gave her head a shake and I said, "You're just putting things together. There's no reason to think Jared was killed at all. No signs. The old man didn't think so."

She said she didn't know what the old man thought, implying I didn't either, but I felt I knew that much. It was simpler to take it all at face value and I could see no reason not to; in fact I may have told myself I refused to, seeing such complexities in any other assumption I would not admit it. I was glad to recall the envelope in his bag and I said to her, "You don't fill out the death certificate of a man you've just done away with." She said don't you? But my mind rejected it, tone, words and thought. I said, "And anyhow, why would that make him want to take us on to Bluffton?"

She studied her hands for a moment. "Suppose he doesn't want you asking these people about him—cop that you are. If he delivers you to Bluffton you couldn't find your way back to save you." I said certainly I could, my car was sitting right at the road to his house. She said, "It may be sitting five miles up or down the highway by the time you see it again."

I said, "Oh, Jo!" and she laughed and waved it all away. "Of course it's fantastic and I don't believe any of it.— Here we are. Which proves how wrong I am. Doesn't it?"

I picked up the manuscript, absurdly enough because the glint of white we saw through the moss and tree trunks was on the far side of the next bend, possibly five minutes away, though maybe less, for we were headed straight at it, slipping along in midstream on the current, or tide, at a good speed, the water muttering under the flat hull. Several buildings were emerging, most of them back from the edge of a low bluff that looked like oyster shells; there was a small white box of a boathouse in a recess in the bluff and some horizontal lines that might have been a short pier. I looked back at Luke; I felt like congratulating him on the achievement of finding it but all I really did was grin and say, "Is this it?"

He leaned forward, not bothering to answer, fished a weathered shingle out of the water that had collected in the bottom and began bailing with one hand, scraping the water up the sides and over in harsh rhythmic scoops that set your teeth on edge.

When I turned round the lines and points had been enlarged to a cluster that showed a bright-colored car under the trees and beyond it a shape that might have been the rear of a station wagon; a low green bateau not very different from ours was slanted against the bank and a white-and-brown speedboat swung out downstream on a line from the end of the dock. Another building appeared and a red convertible like an ember in a bed of ashes. I asked Jo if she saw any life about the place, an idle question in this day when you can tell at once whether anybody is at home by a glance at the garage; I didn't see anybody but I knew people were there and the picture looked as gay as a festival to me, all the brighter for the wilderness-frame it sat in.

The river was a lot wider now than when we had started and the current was less, as if we were nearing sea level, and coming from behind the screen of the point I saw that the woods broke off a few hundred yards beyond the buildings and opened into one of those great marshy clearings that had been rice fields in colonial times; below it the woods took up again but in between you could make out the low dikes and the uprights of watergates by which they had been flooded, and still were in the duck season. I said over my shoulder, hating to take my eyes from it, "Who owns this place?"—in other words, how do I address these people? these beautiful people who will be leaning off their dock to give us a hand up, reaching down for fiddles and heavy brown water-stained package. I had more than paid for my passage but I thought in the joy of deliverance I would hand the Indian ten dollars more. Ten? Maybe twenty.

We were almost abreast of the dock and when I realized we were still out in midstream I looked behind me, partly because he hadn't answered, though I was getting used to that by now, and partly because I had asked myself in an incredulous flash what did I do if he really didn't want to land us? not serious about it but in a habit you get into from writing fiction when you may consider momentarily all kinds of impossible alternatives, just to be sure you are covering the field. He was sitting there impassively, narrow right hand on the steering handle, gazing across at the buildings.

I was about to say something when I remembered from some place that you came alongside a landing with your bow into the current and though that seemed ridiculous in a little skiff like ours I waited a minute or two longer to let him get below and then make the turn. Nothing changed, neither our course nor the full throttle of the motor, and I said, "Pull in," sitting about sideways on the seat.

She put her hand on my knee. "He's not going to land us. But I've got another idea."

I said, "Pull in! This is where I want to land."

He didn't take his eyes off the river, made no move at all, said nothing until I found myself on my feet in the bilgewater and he said, "Sit down, Mister, you'll upset the boat."

It left me speechless like a not-quite-clear message of disaster, an emergency telegram with some words left out. There were two people on the dock watching us now, a tall man and a woman in a yellow sweater. I made a wild gesture with my arms, trying to indicate something of our situation, thinking of the speedboat, I suppose, and how they could easily overtake us if they moved quickly. The woman waved a careless salute that recalled the engineer, the man watching with his hands in his pockets and making a turn toward the house. I said, "Don't you understand? We want to land here."

He said, "You can't land there. Those ain't friendly people. If you go overboard, Mister, I don't guarantee to get you."

If we had had the gun I would have pointed it, foolish as that would have been, he sitting there with the pistol butt showing under the Army coat. I sat down facing him. "Land us here below the house," I said, for we were drifting past it at a surprising speed. "You can be gone before anybody sees you."

"There ain't time to stop. I can hardly make Bluffton by first dark as it is."

It occurred to me he might be holding out for money and I said, "I'll pay you extra. It'll take you five minutes and I'll give you twenty-five dollars."

He said, "You want your car fixed, don't you?" and I said, "I'll take care of that. You just put us ashore." He said, "You can get a mechanic in Bluffton. He'll go with you and fix it for you."

I changed my tone, or maybe the tone changed itself as I began to see the possibility of being unable to persuade him. "I don't have time to go to Bluffton, Luke. I have to get this package on a plane that leaves at six-fifteen. If you'll turn back quickly these people will help me. I can just make it. That was the bargain."

"I don't know anything about any bargain."

"The old man said if I'd help him with Jared he'd take me to somebody with a car."

"Mr. Boyce is getting old. He wasn't up to coming so he asked me to bring you, that's all I know."

"All right. You've brought us. Let us out." He spit over the side again as if that were reply enough. I suddenly thought of saying, "You know the penalty for kidnaping." It surprised him and I was encouraged to go on. "You're heading straight into serious trouble. When you hold people against their will it's kidnaping," not at all sure it was but believing I sounded convincing.

He said, "Nobody's holding you. I'm trying to help you get your car fixed."

I said, "Well, put us ashore!" my voice coming up. We were almost past the rice fields by now, the woods beginning to gather ahead again as if to renew a grip; behind, the buildings had sunk back into the moss, nothing much left but a few strips of fading white. I saw his quick eyes glance toward the bank and I thought for the first time his determination might waver. He said, "You wouldn't want to land over there."

I told him to swing round and take us up just above the rice fields. "Let us out at the lower end of the bluff." I felt her hand on my arm through a sort of semi-consciousness, knowing it was there but disregarding the fact in my exasperation, for he made no move to change the course. We continued our way, following the midstream current, and I knew argument wasn't getting me anywhere. The flap of his holster appeared to be buttoned down, as if he had given no thought to it at all, and I started adding this to the fact of his being hardly more than four feet away, and I wondered if a sudden jump at him might not tip him clean over the stern. It was still his right hand on the steering handle; he would have to change it to his left hand, reach across himself with his right, snatch at the button of the holster. I didn't think he could do it as quickly as I could fall on him; I could bring the boat around, haul him in and be back at the plantation in ten minutes or maybe less.

It wasn't her hand that held me back; I suppose it was my past, my lifetime of non-violence. You lose the trick of primitive action. You think first, and of such things as whether the man might drown, whether both of you might go over, whether in the struggle you might swamp the boat. By the time I had weighed three things that might go wrong he had shifted the grip to his left hand and it was too late, and I turned about on the seat and faced the wind, defeated, despising all thinking, her words running through the back of my mind about what happened if it didn't make the plane—it wouldn't affect what's in here—trying to touch some sort of bottom, some limit to the defeat.

"Listen," she said. "I've got another idea."

117

I sat there looking at my clenched fists, more angry at myself than anyone else yet angry too at the circumstances that had piled up one on another to trap me. If I had gone round on the other road as Cloud had suggested there would have been cars passing; none of this would have happened. Or if I had stayed with the car. Or if I had gone back to it. Every time, the wrong turn. Until now there were no turns left to choose from.

"You're not listening."

"That was the last chance," I said. I didn't want to hear any more adolescent theories about art and quality and the good life. This book was written for publishing and publishing now. It wasn't a matter of how good it was; it was good enough. Maybe it wasn't all I should have liked—whether she had given me that idea or had opened up one I already had—but it was the best I was capable of. Under the circumstances. And I could hear her saying *what* circumstances?

She said, "Listen. We can rent a car in Bluffton."

"What the hell good would it be to rent a car in Bluffton? It'll be five o'clock before we get there." Then I remembered she wouldn't know the geography and I gathered patience enough to tell her Bluffton was on the other side of the Sound. "It must be fifty miles from my car. You couldn't possibly—"

"Maybe so, but not fifty from the airport."

I opened my hands and looked at the raw skin without noticing it. She put her hand on my wrist and leaned forward; I guess it was pretty obvious I was listening. "We'll fix our car later. Fix it tomorrow, any old time. We'll go straight to the field. What's to stop it?"

I had got used to deadends. I searched for the deadend of that. Costly, troublesome, a makeshift, but I couldn't see a deadend. It couldn't have been more than twenty miles from Bluffton to the airport. I looked at her and the diamond-shaped smile. "If you're really determined to get it on board, that ought to do it."

I said, "That ought to do it," repeating her words more than saying it, a ꜱort of incredulous peace beginning to spread through me, through my resisting wariness. Another chance? As if somebody had been saying, last chance, you bitched it, you're lost, that's all, oh give the poor bastard another chance. It had been happening all day. All day? All my life. Or rather since the death of Christ. I said, "That ought to do it. I don't see why not." No trouble getting a car, it was a going town; then off over the long bridges and the marshes to Waltonville and left on the causeway and the drawbridge to Jasmine Island—jess'min, for Cape jess'min (my mother's word for gardenia) or maybe for yellow jess'min, but a fragrant word in any case. Then and now. I said, "We could leave Bluffton as late as a quarter to six."

"Why not?"

And I finally agreed to accept it. "By God, Jo, that's something!" leaning over and pressing my face against her hand. "You have a book dedicated to you, Josephine. 'To Josephine Seeley, for a happy landing.' 'To Jo, who, with Bach, managed a happy landing.' I'll think of something."

I expected more response than one of her short intake-laughs, and I said after a minute, "But maybe you'd rather read it first." She said she somehow doubted if it was her book, not in a mean way but coolly enough to reduce some of my exuberance. After a while she said without much apparent sequence, "Does environment make much difference to you, Wesley?"

I gazed round in an ironic survey of the woods and the

clouds and the widening black river, about to say that this one did, but before I could speak she said, "I don't mean this. What I really mean is what sort of environment were you in when you wrote *All the Month of March?*"

I remembered well enough but I didn't much care about going into it; I didn't think it had been an important angle of the book. I have written books in too many different surroundings to think environment is a controlling element; contributing, possibly, but if I couldn't write a book in Manhattan I shouldn't expect to be able to write it in Acapulco. I told her there was no one environment for making a book.

She said, "But don't you think there may be one that's rightest for you?"

I told her I had written a book in an office on the fourteenth floor of a building on Forty-second Street and I had written a book in the bedroom of a boarding house in Beaufort, South Carolina. She said which was better? and I said I didn't know, wondering whether I would go into the delicate question of what we meant by better. Before I could decide she said, "*All the Month of March* doesn't sound like either place."

I said, "I wrote it, or most of it, in a men's dormitory one summer at the University of Wisconsin."

She said, "Well!"

I thought she was adding up the facts that the book was written five or six years ago and I was hardly of an age then when you would expect to find me in a dormitory at a college summer school. She said, "You know what the obstetrician said to the squalling new baby. 'When you were in you wanted out, now you're out you want in.' Or were you on the faculty? Giving a short-story course?" I told her I was a student, putting together again the way

I had felt that spring, dissatisfied with a book I had just finished and looking round for a clean break of some kind, my eyes turning to the mirage of Europe. "I happened on a newspaper photograph of one J. Sam Shaw (I remember the name very well) in cap and gown getting a Masters in music at the age of eighty-four. My forty-six didn't feel so heavy." That was about the first of June. By the middle Livia was on the way to France and I was on the way to Wisconsin.

"What did you take?"

"Anthropology or algebra or something like that. What I remember most about it was that it began at quarter to eight. The rabbits and robins and chipmunks would hardly get out of the path to let me by. I flunked the course, but I was fed well, left completely alone by all the healthy kids—not avoided, just ignored, the way you might be walking through a pasture of grazing cows too hungry to even look up from the beautiful clover. I forgot there was such a thing as a bottle of liquor. My age didn't embarrass me. It was sort of a magic cloak; I could see them but they couldn't see me. I found myself writing six, seven, eight hours a day; of course I had had the book in my head for a long time." I stopped talking but my mind went on with it, with the many other things I saw or thought I saw, tying it all up with undergraduate days a quarter-century gone until I was practically eating and sleeping and shaving with ghosts of myself, unrecognizable in costume, Lord knows, but betrayed by their hopes and expectations. It wouldn't have surprised me in the least to hear somebody say all he wanted in this world was to write one good book. And ghosts of the teachers too, or rather of the earnestness and integrity, an actual family likeness between the two generations of professors, the way they walked and stood, their fingering of a piece of chalk, as if respect for books were itself a powerful gene—all of it, what I saw and what I read into it, leaving me with a sense of these places, like the monasteries in the Dark Ages, nursing the seeds of our civilization in the new darkness gathering.

"Why don't you try it again?"

"As I told you, the book sold three thousand copies."

"You said six."

"I said *less* than six—which is three. And also, my scholastic record makes my welcome there something a little short of cordial."

"Can't you find some university where your disgrace is not known?"

I told her they had their ways of tracking you down.

She fell silent, the smile dying out of her face. "All I know is a person has got to speak in his own voice. He makes it as good as he knows how, sometimes better than he knows how, but good or bad, that's what he's got to stand on. Now me, I don't know what my voice is."

"I think you know very well. You're a top-grade musician."

"I'm just a wandering fiddler."

"The hell you say."

She smiled down at the canvas overcases and rubbed at a smear on one of them that hadn't been there this morning. "And all this damp is not doing my fiddles any good." I asked her when she was expected to show up at the hotel and she said, "Cocktail music five-thirty to six-thirty, dinner music seven to eight-thirty, dance music nine to eleven," not answering the question exactly but certainly letting it sound as if she needed to be there by five, knew she would be late and didn't set much store by it. It seemed to take care of the little quandary that had been stirring in my head earlier of how we were to separate; I would drop her there when we left the field, probably go on back to Waltonville for the night. I had long since lost interest in my pompano. It also took care of the other question that had been plaguing me off and on; I didn't know what these kids expected. Chastity wasn't what it used to be and I had wondered if, safely out of all this mess, politeness might not call for me to propose bed as well as board. I didn't know, and I was glad now I shouldn't have to know; I have enjoyed my increasing powers of talking back to Sex. It can't shove me around any more.

I said, "You're too good for that kind of music," and she laughed. "I know I am. That's the difference between you and me. I know when I'm too good for something and I'll get out of it at the very first chance."

I said I didn't know where she picked up these ideas about me. "Somebody who knew me very well once told me I had Little Magazine tastes and mass-media talents."

"Zonk! You must have made her awfully mad."

"She was pretty mad."

"Bitch."

"But I'm not sure she wasn't about right."

"So you sat down and wrote a book to prove it?"

I said, "Look, I think, honestly, this 'bitch' was closer to being right than you are. If you don't have what it takes, the question is do you do the job you can do or do you keep butting your head against a wall trying to do a job that's beyond you?"

"How can you ask such a stupid question? You keep butting the wall of course."

"Why not accept your limitations?"

"For the simple reason they're not your limitations until you accept them. If you think this book is inferior—"

"I didn't say that."

"But if you thought so, the very fact that you thought so would mean you could visualize something better. If you can ask the question, you know, you're halfway to answering it. You know what I think, Wesley?"

I told her I was beginning to have a pretty good idea.

"I believe a person has a much wider influence all round him than he thinks he has. A chain influence, others on others on others. You don't have to be conscious of it; maybe it's better not to be, then your brain doesn't interfere. Somebody with courage gives you courage, just hearing about him. Somebody without, it's the other way." She waited a minute then said quietly, "Pa's sister killed herself, Aunt Josie. No particular reason anybody could see. In fact she had taken care of Grandpa for years and then he died and she was free for the first time to do what she wanted to, go where she pleased. And she killed herself. I didn't know her very well. I'm not blaming her, I'm just saying I'm different because she did it. I'll always be a little scareder.—And always trying to act as if I wasn't."

"You're not scared."

"I'm not as scared as I was before we buried Jared. That old man was—the only word I can think of is steadfast. And I'm a little more steadfast now too. Not much," she gave her brief gasp of a laugh, "but some. And you didn't flinch either, Wesley."

"Didn't I!" But I was pleased she said it and pleased when she said, "It didn't show. If you can raise yourself a little it raises a lot of other people. Whatever the scientists say, we're a long way from being just animals and that's how it has happened. That's why the so-called 'finer things of life' are important, they have a slight effect on helping you grow away from being just an animal. As if a person's main purpose here was to work himself a little further away from being just an animal, and by getting himself a little further away give other people courage to do the same thing. That's why you have to keep butting the wall. The just-animals haven't learned how to do that yet."

I said, "What do you want me to do with this box, throw it in the river?"

I thought she might smile but she didn't, looking away at the farther bank, the river getting wider now, tide-level marks following every indentation like lines on a contour map. She said, "I'm going to give myself the benefit of all doubts. If there is some doubt as to whether I've got talent or have not I'm going to assume I have."

"I love you for saying it, Jo."

She flung out her wrist in a sort of annoyance. "What's the use to assume anything else? If you assume you're good and it turns out you're not I don't see that you're any worse off than if you assume you're second-rate and it turns out you were right. It's no fun telling yourself I told you so. I had a friend in the woodwinds when I was playing in St. Louis once. Every time a man took her to the movies she thought he was getting ready to marry her. She had one boy, worked in a real estate office, good job, who took her out once a week. After a month she told everybody in the band she was getting married. He hadn't asked her. She just *assumed* he would. She told the concert master they had better dig around for another English horn, she would be getting married in a few weeks. We all got worked up about it; we'd stand round at rehearsal waiting to ask her how things were going. I said, 'Is this thing in the bag, Lily? Because if it's not and it falls through you'll feel like a fool for having told everybody.' It fell through. I said, 'You shouldn't have told everybody until you were sure.' She said if she had waited until she was sure she would never have had anything to tell. She had enjoyed telling it, enjoyed everybody being interested, asking her about it. Now that it was all over and nobody paid any special attention to her any more it was no worse than it had been before it all started. If you count your chickens before they hatch at least you do get one chance to count. If they hatch you can count them again." She laughed with the little sucking in of breath through her teeth and I wondered if all this had happened among the woodwinds or among the strings.

I didn't like to ask her, though I guess I did in a backhanded way when I asked if she had hitchhiked from St. Louis to Columbia. But that didn't interest her; she could hold to a subject with an iron grip. "You play them too close, Wesley. You've got to take a chance."

I told her that was one of the differences between her age and mine. "As you get older you accumulate more and more things you don't want to take a chance of losing, position, some reputation, maybe a little income, maybe even a few friends."

"Trash!"

"They make life comfortable and pleasant."

"That's all right for the Philistines. That's all they've got, comfort and pleasure. But an artist can't settle for that. Or maybe if he's an artist his comfort and pleasure get to be a little more complicated than gasoline and alcohol and inner-spring mattresses."

"You put a lot more stock in this artist fellow than most people do."

She smiled but her voice had a ring. "Eyes of the fleet, Wesley," moving her arm above the morose woods in a broad slow sweep of reconnaissance. "He sees it before it happens. Or what he really does is feel it happening before the general run feels any change at all. Cézanne felt a change coming, or his unconscious did. Matisse and Braque were a lot more specific. They showed you the change thirty or forty years before the general run saw anything—new standards, subjectivity, psychoanalysis, the subconscious, confusion of values, tensions."

"You see the artist as some sort of super-being with a private wire to the Almighty."

"No, anybody could see it coming if he was tuned up keen enough. And not fooled into putting all his attention on the intelligence. The artist is watching the instincts and emotions; that's where the future comes from. The intelligence can improve it a little—or disimprove it—but it's just an editor with a blue pencil waiting for the instincts and emotions to send him a manuscript."

"I see your artist as a small forgotten man, confused and ineffective, a caster of spells, a dealer in magic and potions in a world of X-rays and isotopes. The world has left him behind."

She snorted. "If it has it'll have to turn round one day and come back and get him. He's the man with the idea. He's the compass. You don't know which way you're heading until he tells you. It's all very well this glamorizing the laboring man but he'll be standing round with his hands in his overalls unless somebody gives him an idea what to labor at.—You know, Wesley, I think the shrinkers have shrunken us down to a point where we don't expect anything of ourselves beyond a few low galvanic reactions. They've performed a sort of lobotomy on the conscience, a sort of Godectomy; sliced out our old idea of Man as God and sewed us up with Man as Grub. They've made it too damn easy for everybody to act like pigs. Or like fourth-graders with the teacher gone out of the room. God's gone home sick, kids, let's have a ball! We've let them make Prodigal Sons of us, disinherited anyway, nothing to lose: pass the marijuana. But the trouble with all that is it undercuts the civilization. The best civilizations have grown up when people thought well of themselves, respected the past and believed in what could be made of the future, believed in the possibilities of some good in themselves. We just go round saying what bastards we are, and you might as well shoot a dog as call him a bastard. But I wonder if we're as low as we like to think. I'm one hell of a long way from an anthropoid ape."

"I'll go along with that, Josephine."

"We're still fascinated at resembling apes, but what does that prove? It's a one-eyed view; we can't balance it off by seeing if we resemble a more highly developed species than ourselves too. We are suffering from being at the top of the ladder, from being the lead dog with nothing to follow but his own scent. But how'd we get to be so different from these apes? And the differences are more important than the resemblances because they point at the future; the resemblances are of purely antiquarian interest. Just ancestor worship. I don't know how the differences started but you don't have to do more than glance at the cave paintings to see the direction the differences were taking us in, twenty-five thousand years ago. I just mean we haven't been apes in so long we might just about as well never have been. Anyway we might as well forget it. And we're not pigs either." She pulled her coat closer and crossed her arms over it. "I'm getting cold again. What are you going to do about that?"

I told her to face round the other way, which she did

with the easy-flowing motions of the young. She turned up the squirrel collar.

I was getting cold too and it was obvious enough why. The river had widened out to double its first size and the woods that had broken the wind had drawn back beyond strips of marsh. From where we were the sawgrass looked about knee high though I knew it was at least as high as your waist, brown and curved over inland like a scimitar, not from this wind which, without our motion into it, I thought would have been no more than fresh, but from the sum of all the ocean winds that had blown across it and across its forebears. The woods still followed the farther edges of it and here and there sent out small isolated stands of trees where strips of solid ground rose out of the grass. They were not rice fields any more, no dikes or gates, nothing man-made however neglected and ruined, pale birds now taking the place of our dark hawks and buzzards, gulls, I suppose, and terns, banking and skating on the wind as if sporting with it. A pelican crossed above us, sank into the sky like an echo.

# *SIX*

But more responsible for the cold than all this primitive expanse of water-grass-ooze, I thought, was the dampness that hung over it; moved over it, because you could see it above your head passing in thin layers, gray on gray, but so inexhaustible and endless that it seemed to move and hang too. The rough threads of my coat were sprinkled with a smoky net of mist. And down ahead, with the river spreading and the water-tone changing toward a blue-green sea-descended color that reminded you of the claws of fresh-caught crabs, the dampness seemed to press down closer, graying out the few trees that still kept us company.

And then I noticed for the first time a different motion to the boat, a hardly perceptible difference, almost deniable, like a young symptom, a slow deepwater swell and fall; and then grown up and deniable no longer. You could see both shores, one closer than the other and neither of them continuous now, broken into stretched-out links by the mouths of small creeks and bays, but ahead of us the shores seemed to pull away from each other and I saw that the layers of dampness overhead were really the fringes of a fog bank. Straight on there was no shore at all, blue-green floor smudging upward into gray ceiling, a porous curtain that reminded me of the woods this morning in the way it seemed to draw backward as you came nearer. Looking directly into it, into all the layers of it, I told myself it must appear denser than it was; and hoped I was right. It had the dirty color of a mid-season circus tent, with none of the festive connotations, filled indeed with a vast silent menace—a menace that was a good deal more specific for me than the classic foreboding naturally a part of these ancient things because no matter how many times the Indian might have made the trip to Bluffton he couldn't find his way blindfolded. And even if the fog blew in no heavier it had a way of changing the look and feel of the world you could see, changing, I was sure, the marks and signs he might remember, the scale of them; I could hardly imagine anyone so experienced he could follow a course through all the confusion of salt creeks and estuaries and backwaters with which that coast eases itself into the ocean. I looked round at him. "Do you have a compass?"

He was holding out to Jo a wide-top Mason jar, shaking it insistently, his broad mouth in a grin that was not so much unpleasant as alien; you somehow knew it had ranged in its time on scrubby pastures. "Central heating," he said. It was about half full of a colorless liquid that foamed into a white bead as he shook it; he may have brought it down to that level himself but he didn't seem drunk. "Doctor's orders."

She accepted it as easily as if it had been a bottle of Coca-Cola, sniffed it with a jerk backward of her head that he accepted as praise and swallowed some. She handed the jar to me, eyes blinking. It was bad to smell and strong and rough but it went down through my chest with blessing and absolution. There was no reservation in my voice when I thanked him; it burned away all I held against him. He shook it and lifted it up with a fatherly pride. "Look how it holds it." He took a flowing familiar drink, smacked his lips, then capped the jar and set it on the bottom beside the lantern.

I pointed ahead and he said indifferently, "May get a little fog before night." I started to ask him again about a compass but changed my mind; I knew he didn't have one. I wasn't sure how much good one would have done anyway.

Fog or not, it was obvious the overcast was going to bring us an early dark. My watch showed only about four-twenty but the light was noticeably weaker, a blue-gray light close kin to the water and clouds, the sort of light that sometimes spreads out before a shower of rain and brightens when the rain passes, leaving the day not so far gone as you had believed. But I didn't think this one would brighten; there were too many layers between us and what was left of the sun out there behind us somewhere packed away without a trace like a jewel in a box of folded cotton, layers that seemed to have also the insulating quality of batts of glass wool or cellulose.

At this time of year it usually gets dark on that coast, headlights-dark, by six; I thought the overcast might push that up half an hour earlier today, not much more than that. Which meant, even with the fog, we ought to be able to reach Bluffton before night. There was nothing I could do anyway but hope; I couldn't speed up the motor. It gave off the same sound it had all afternoon and I supposed it was wide open, but even if he had reduced it or should have to reduce it later if the fog closed in, he was going to do what he pleased, as we had already discovered. And I couldn't find us a short cut; in fact I couldn't be sure in what direction Bluffton lay, more or less straight ahead I guessed, granting he wasn't lost, somewhere between us and the ocean. And granting we weren't a lot closer to the ocean than we thought we were.

I turned my back to the wind, to the immensities in it as much as to the cold, picking up the manuscript beside me and pushing about on plaster-cast legs, then taking the dirty wad of handkerchief out of my breast pocket and wiping the brown paper. There was a film of moisture over the box as over everything else, face, misbegotten hat (misgotten, anyway), necktie, to my stained trouser-cuffs, and wiping it smeared Graham's name into a hopeless streak; this was of no matter because I would be able to readdress it at the field, but the damp was not doing the wrapping any good, the top. The bottom was pretty dry. I blotted up the wet with the handkerchief and tossed it in the river. It whipped away and was gone before my eyes.

We were sliding along (I thought he *had* cut the speed) within throwing distance of a shelving oyster bank, the bone-white of it breaking off evenly into the black band where the tide had pulled away. You could see the real height of the marshgrass now, rising up way above our heads in the graceful gentle scimitar-bend that was as misleading as the grace of a tiger. I remembered reading of a military prisoner trying to escape through such grass from Parris Island and being found next day by helicopter half dead and bleeding from a thousand slashes. We were close enough to see the tide streaming outward past the bank and I asked the Indian how far we were from the ocean, tried to ask it in an easy voice as if the idea of being carried out to sea had never occurred to me. He said it was a long way to the ocean, which made me feel better. I said, "Which way is Bluffton? What direction?"

He straightend out all fingers of his free hand, taking his time, and pointed diagonally across the open water.

It was not where I expected. I had thought it was ahead, the way we were going, though I should have remembered it was on the other side. I said, "Do we have to cross that?" He said farther down, and I said, "Why didn't you cross upstream, where it wasn't so wide?" There was wind enough to roughen any large piece of water into waves that would come over our freeboard, in places hardly a foot.

"Shorter this way."

I had no answer to it. Maybe it was. There had been a map of the "drainage basin" on the wall of the cottage but I hadn't given it any attention beyond occasional detached glances at Little North Forks and South Branches and Cuts and Reaches and "rivers" that weren't rivers but watery passes round the backs of islands and hammocks—"Rabbit Island," "Little Mud River," "Honeygal Creek"—my eye had swept over all of them without the faintest tremor of forecast. But I remembered the curls and windings now, and what would be the shorter way or the longer was beyond me. I thought I should rather have gone the longer way than make this crossing in the twilight with a fog bank drifting in, but it was too late for that now; and maybe back there I would have taken the short way, with the time running out. We were already moving in a sort of broad flat-bottomed hemisphere, nothing at all ahead after the water faded out in a few hundred yards, and noticing it only now, I saw that the fog had accumulated behind us and had absorbed all the farther woods completely; you could still make out signs of one shore for perhaps a quarter of a mile. I had been thinking the fog was all in front of us but we had been moving through it for probably five or ten minutes. It reminded me of my last birthday when for some reason I happened to see that age was not just something for tomorrow; I had been moving through it for some time.

And it reminded me too of something else, another one of those impalpable accumulations. How long had I been moving through these doubts—about the book but also about my direction, which the book really epitomized? Though "how long" was not the point; what I meant was that the doubts were denser round me than I had realized. I used to wonder, at a more speculative age, about the "change-over" points, where one substance apparently changes and becomes quite something else; the point where rainwater in the tree roots becomes sap in the trunk, where the decaying vegetation becomes the coal. If it changed, there must have been a minute point at which it ceased being one thing and became the other; the point at which the food we eat becomes the idea, the point at which the hypothesis becomes the dogma. And this seemed, not trivial, but very important to me because the alternative to supposing that one thing became another, which you could hardly grant, was to grant that there had always been something of the second thing in the first and that there was merely an increase and decrease, and not a change-over, which necessitated assuming a startling inter-relationship that extended all the way to saying there was something of death in life and that life did not suddenly change into death but merely decreased in its concentration until there was very little, but always some, of it left. And not just material life but to the other one too, the person himself, the life that existed round and through the material life. To the reasoners, that was supposed to end, but if one didn't end, did the other? Did it change into death or, like the first, somehow become only *more* dead? until maybe the death in turn declined and the life increased again. Heresy? Well, heresy.—Which made me say you don't put meaning into your life but reveal (if you can!) the meaning already there. And also made me say if I had doubts about this book now, about the direction I was going, I must always have had them; it strengthened my respect for them, my being comfortable with them. They were mine, not someone else's; cultivated by someone else, perhaps (or rather, certainly), but not planted.

Of course the question really in my mind was could I do any better? Not do any better if I wanted to but if, as the phrase goes, my life depended on it? Maybe, as I had said, this was as good a book as I could write. Certainly a man would have such a limit; somewhere. Not where he thought, possibly, but somewhere. The question was where? How could you tell? There were no doubt scientific tests that would give you an answer true in a majority of cases, but there was that minority of which every man considered himself a member; you might be one of the exceptions, in fact you would know very well you were. Actually, for me, it came down to whether I was going to believe a sophisticated adult woman who had known me day and night for six years or a young romantic who had known me for a few hours—though the young one, with so much time ahead, would probably say I had to torment myself trying, whether I could or couldn't. But what possible harm was there in accepting a success like this? Already in your hand. It wasn't as if I were facing a blank page and deciding between writing a first-grade book and a second-grade. I was willing to grant (what with her pounding) this was probably not a top job; something less, watered down. Not much but some. But suppose it was? There would be a next time and next time there wouldn't have to be a watering down. Wouldn't be; I thought I could say that. Agree with her or not (as it was between her and her namesake aunt, but in reverse), it would never be the same as if I hadn't known her. Not that she had taught me, but reminded me. Next time I would be remembering Josephine—or rather, Jo—instead of remembering Livia.

But I hadn't really been remembering Livia. This book was only negligibly Livia. By the time I left New York with it it was more Carlotta than Livia. And even months before, when I asked Tom Dukes to read two hundred pages, about half of it as it turned out, it was quite different. I remembered the glint on his glasses as he rocked back in his editorial chair because the vast new cliff of Madison Avenue windows behind his head was glinting in the same way, the manuscript out there between us in two almost equal piles; it was January, almost a year ago exactly, afternoon and getting dark deep down in the arroyo, though a sparking city dark, not this deadly night. "Here's what they mean, Bill, and you can take it or leave it. We'll publish it as it stands if that's the way you want it." He had got two other readings on it but he didn't want to tell me who they were and I didn't care anyhow. "They want some more details, and I think they are right. They feel if you add a few pages in here and few pages in a couple of other places I've marked it will make all the difference between having a possible hit and having a ringer. I don't mean pornography. Just some more details; carry it all a little further. You draw the curtain on these two at exactly the time when a hundred thousand readers are going to feel cheated. Tastes change. It used to be enough to have a few bedroom scenes but the modern reader expects some bed scenes, what with inflation and all," laughing and turning up his hand.

I said I didn't mind putting them to bed but I felt the subject had been pretty well worked over lately; I didn't see what I could tell that hadn't been already told. I said, "The closer you get to the sheets the less individuality there is to write about." He said, "Okay, Bill, I just wanted to pass on the gist of these two reports. Whatever you want to do about it is all right." He paused to give a little laugh, watching his hand turn a pencil end over end on his blotter, then said, "But it hasn't all been written, Bill. I could give you a phone number—no, I won't do any such thing. You handle it in your own way."

I got the number from him of course but I don't think he will be giving it to any more of his people; for a while, six or seven months, it looked like good-bye, book. And good riddance. It was four months or so before I could write a line, that is, anything except letters to the lady, two- and three-thousand-word letters and almost daily, written morning or noon or night, whenever I wasn't with her (she had certain commitments), written in ecstasy and agony, singing and wailing and moping. I suppose they were the adult equivalent of the interminable teen-age phone conversations that parents complain of, but the letters became the center of my life, hell with the book, the letters and Carlotta herself, one supplementing the other, it seems to me now, the letters charged with what I hadn't been able to get into words when I had been with her, and when I was with her again the intervening letter had set up all kinds of tensions that had to be resolved, the resolving of which produced another letter.

Of course it wasn't very long, I am a little ashamed to

138

confess, before my professional eye began to suspect that these were wonderful letters; they were thrown off mostly in pencil or pen or both on the first scrap of paper that came to hand and I had no way of rereading them in tranquility—granting tranquility could have been come by—but now and then she quoted something in them, read a few lines back to me. She was a very intelligent young woman, not intellectual, not literary, but highly sensitive to shades of emotion, responsive, not always as I had foreseen but responsive. I think the letters amazed her. I know they did me, and I tried for some time after the first few weeks, desperately I might almost say, to keep a carbon. But writing them on the typewriter, which I tried, took something out of them and when I tried making a carbon in longhand it wasn't much better; it was a little like talking over a phone you know is tapped. I gave it up. I dare say I had it in mind that one day—one sad day, and yet not so sad because I sometimes longed for my pre-Carlotta peace—she would throw them all in my face and I would have the originals.

An alternative to that disturbed me for a while though not for long, which was the idea that conceivably her lawyer might some day be reading these letters aloud before judge and jury unless I came across with more than I could come across with, that she might even sell them for a nice sum to one of the confession magazines. Or threaten to. But I saw as soon as I examined it that that was ridiculous, not that she might not do it but that it represented a threat. You can't blackmail a writer with the threat of publishing his work. My only real worry was that I had no copies and that she might not, for any one of a number of reasons, toss over the real thing.

Which of course was what happened. I had begun to

come to my senses again, some time in late August I think
("regain consciousness" Dukes called it afterward with
more understanding than sympathy), when she turned to
me one night as we walked out of the Oak Room at the
Plaza and asked me if I was going to miss her. I said,
"You're going out of town?" I thought she might have
made some plans for the Labor Day weekend that didn't
include me and I was really rather glad to think she might
have. I like holidays in the city. She said, "Didn't I tell
you?" lifting her beautiful eyebrows in what I spotted
quite readily by that stage was phony surprise. I said, "Tell
me what?" and she said, "Darling, I'm going to Spain tomorrow."

I think I took it fairly well, I hope so. It was consider-
ably more than I had bargained for. In any case I had hold
of myself well enough not to ask her who she was going
with. In the hall outside her apartment as she probed purse
for key I said with I thought a successful front of offhandedness that all those ridiculous old notes of mine,
rather than burn them herself she might just give them
back to me to burn. She looked at me with the key frozen
to her fingers. "Give them back, Bill! What do you mean?"
I said, "I mean I'll get rid of them. I've got a fireplace, you
know, and you haven't."

"But they're mine, Darling."

I said well, they were mine too in a way and she said,
"No, mine only. *I made you write them*," spacing out the
words with little icicles between them.

It was several weeks more before I could keep my head
above water with any consistency, but one blessed day my
feet touched bottom and I waded dripping ashore. I was
cured but I wasn't the Bill Johns of January; I felt as if my
head had been shaved and treated with a permanent depila-

tory. But the peace that descended on me was the one you feel at being dismissed from the hospital after major surgery; the world was new. I finished the book in less than a month, not to my satisfaction but giving it the over-all shape it was to have; there were some holes in it with outlines thrown over them, and Graham wanted some holes where there weren't any. Tom Dukes called up the care-taker; I got the car out of dead storage in White Plains, bought a new battery and headed south.

For me the plantation was a convalescent home. Solitude was my tonic. The changes I made in the script may not have been exactly what the two readers had had in mind but they went in that direction; I found I could piece out some of the letters from memory, helped by the half-dozen penciled notes in Carlotta's irregular but firm hand (open-ing without salutation and ending without name or initial) and I fitted them in, smoothed out the joints. I talked to Tom long-distance after he had seen a hundred-page hunk in final shape. "That does it!" he said. I was very pleased. I told him to ship it back so I could get the whole picture. He said, "Okay, Bill, but when are you going to cut loose from this thing? Graham's getting worried." We fixed a date. I overran it; I was having more trouble cutting Graham's copy down to length than writing the whole book. I got an ultimatum, then an ulti-ultimatum—on which I now had, I figured, thirty-five minutes' grace, allowing five minutes between the Bluffton waterfront and the garage or taxi stand from which we would zoom away.

I said to Dr. Indian over there squinting down the river at the soft view as if trying to keep smoke out of his eyes, "How far is it from the dock at this place to where I can grab a car? I mean how long will it take me?"

He had never been a quick one for answering and I supposed he was turning it over in his mind how long a walk it was, maybe whose garage he would send me to, how much of a kickback he could count on; he took a good while then he said, "I thought maybe you'd want to come with me to hand in the papers on Jared."

I wanted to shout deliver me! but I said, "I'll leave that to you. No reason for me to come."

"No sir, but we're all in this together and I thought—"

I said, "Look, I'm not in this at all. I just happened to be passing by." At exactly the wrong moment I almost said but didn't. He said something about I had helped with the burial and I said, "I only did it as a favor to the old man. He thought you might not be back for days. I'm not in it at all."

He said, "Yes sir, we're all in it," and I said what did he mean? getting a funny feeling in my stomach. He said, "On the certificate where it calls for who buried him I put your name down with Mr. Boyce. Had to."

I had forgotten he knew my name though I shouldn't have, writing it out for him myself. But beyond the surprise of this was the annoyance of being implicated to that extent. Yet even that extent didn't strike me as any reason I should take the time to go with him to file the report; or any reason, as I thought of it, that he should suggest it.

Then he said, and I began to see what it was all about and it left me without much further comment, except to myself trying to straighten out where I stood, "I wouldn't want you to go off thinking something was wrong without understanding you're in it too."

"How am I in it!"

"Helping conceal the body, Mr. Johns. That is if anything was wrong."

And there it was at last. We were on our way to Bluffton to let me see my name fed into the records, to let me be sure to understand that if he was guilty I was guilty; that the only way I could get immunity was to grant him immunity too. It was a breathtaking stepping up of my troubles and I fumbled round for some way out of it, any way. I'm not a brother's-keeper sort of man, not a meddler. I don't go digging into other people's guilt or innocence if I can help it; I have enough guilt and innocence of my own to unravel. I said, "Wrong? What could be wrong?"

He said, "I don't see anything wrong," and I took a big breath and let it out and said, "I don't either."

I was sick of the whole thing, of the box, of what was inside it, of the fantastic chain of unmerited troubles one little accident had released. Sick of the too-obvious fact that the chain was still unwinding. And sick of this down-the-riverness, on and on, one hope growing into its death and into the birth of a new hope, and that dying and leaving a new hope behind, all of it too much like a giant metaphor for my taste, implacable rudder-man steering as he would what I had been and what I was, and what I might be too. There was no sign of Bluffton, or sound. I thought, once, I heard a foghorn on a twist of the wind but there was no reason to believe it was located at Bluffton. And even if it was, there was no encouragement to be drawn from the fact; a foghorn might carry five miles, maybe ten on a wind like that, packed so close with damp-ness—so close I couldn't tell when it turned to rain, a veil of rain that swept lightly across the back of my neck, brushed down the side of my face like a chilly cobweb. I thought if some good (or evil) spirit had offered to lift me out of there into a warm dry room at the sacrifice of the manuscript I would have thrown it out in the black water before he finished offering. I tried to button it inside my coat but it was too thick.

As I groped about with it, stiff-fingered, she reached across me, took hold of the cord and heaved it into her lap. She unbuttoned the top of the wide cloth coat that had seemed so grotesque back in the other life of traffic-lights and gasoline pumps and stored the box away inside; the russet cases, or a good part of them, were already there. I nodded my thanks. I said I hoped all this was not going to ruin her instruments.

"They're waterproof cases."

"If it does we'll buy you some new ones, charge it against royalties."

"New ones!" I hadn't expected thanks but I wasn't prepared for scorn either. I said, "Well, we'll find you some new old ones then," but she shook her head. "These are used to me. Know my faults."

"They sound like dogs."

"Cats. Fiddles like to be round people, the way cats do. Fiddles are funny." She gazed a minute at the wet bottom of the boat and went on, "Back in the Seventeenth Century some rich nobles bought up a lot of Strads. They didn't know anything about them except they were valuable and they figured they would get a lot more valuable after Mr. Strad died. They stored them away in vaults, everything just right, not too damp, not too dry, even temperature. But when their children took them out, or their great-grandchildren I guess, years later, a century or so, they sounded like something you'd get at Sears Roebuck. They had to be played again for a long time before they came back, years and years. They hadn't been round people in so long they had got wild. Like the cats in the Forum," pausing for a little smile at a button of the coat.

"It takes years of playing to make a fiddle. And not just sawing, that's the funny part. Once somebody tested a couple of new violins, good ones, just alike or practically. He put one on a machine that sawed back and forth on the strings for a thousand hours; the other one he got a good violinist to take home and practice on for six months. No comparison how much better the second one sounded. A fiddle will go on improving for ten years if it's played right. A beginner can improve a fiddle in the lower positions and not be able to break it in in the higher ones. It will sound better low than high unitl somebody good breaks in the highs too."

She looked round at me over the top of the hunched-up collar, nothing showing but forehead, eyes, nose, an ear, a thin-skinned cheek, and I noticed for the first time they were delicate well-made features, all of them aglow from what she had been saying. It seemed to me her face had responded to the ardor playing over it like her reclaimed violins, and the realization came to me with something of a shock that she was almost beautiful.

I told her I felt very bad to have got her into all this. I think I felt worse at the thought I should soon be seeing the last of her, a most appealing person somehow, over all the wastes between us. "But maybe it will teach you you had better use some other kind of transportation."

She looked off with the diamond smile and said, "Give up hitching?" In a minute the smile seemed to die out, though the diamond was still there, and she said in the quiet tone of merely reporting what she had already said to herself, "It's the most wonderful hitch I've ever had." I said, "You think so?" and she said, "I've never been as unhappy in my life as I am this minute but when it's all over it will get more wonderful every day."

I scraped up enough humor or irony or something to say, "So glad you could come."

I didn't repeat her "when it's all over," adding an exclamation point, which was what I felt like doing but I must have transmitted it somehow because she said, "I guess you're not happy either. And you must be cold," glancing at me and my turned-up collar and my borrowed hat that had long since come to seem my own. She moved closer and offered me her arm, which I took hesitantly, hating to show myself weakly shivering as I was. But I must have transmitted that too for she said, "I wonder if the good doctor has used up all the tonic," and lifted her head and signaled.

The little ritual of holding up the jar and shaking it showed me more than the fact there were hardly three fingers of it left; it showed me how the night had fallen since he had shaken it last. I could just make out the band of white bubbles. Beyond him, up the river (or up the bay, or where the hell ever we were), the wall of marsh-grass was almost indistinguishable now at its closest, and I thought in a swift wave of depression that came and went like a gust of the fine rain that dying might be something like this, sliding along in a growing dark and fog and cold, some other agency at the controls, malign or not you weren't quite sure but certainly imperturbable, asking you nothing, no decisions needed or wanted or of any value, no use in trying to act even if you knew an act to try. She took a good swallow from the jar and I did the same.

But I was hardly conscious of taking it, for the other aspect of all this that rose up in my mind. It was almost dark. In fifteen or twenty minutes you wouldn't be able to see the length of the boat. We either got to Bluffton, or in sight of it, within a quarter of an hour or (I could hardly say it) we didn't get there at all, or rather, not to exaggerate it, we didn't get there until daybreak. Once dark had come you might creep up and down in this maze all night. The lantern was no good to us—except maybe as a signal—which he evidently realized for he seemed to have no intention of lighting it.

Of course, I told myself, the danger was scarcely anything more than that; we would get there eventually. We might run short of gas but there would be shrimp boats out at daylight. There wasn't much chance of being washed out to sea because the tide would be turning in an hour or two. There was no sign of any strong blow developing. But all the reassurances I could think of added up to nothing, to dropping in pebbles to fill a well; all night in the boat, or even huddled on the slope of one of the oyster banks—

I said, "Which way do you figure Bluffton is now?" largely to make him say something, that we were almost there or it wouldn't be long or anything to keep up some communication, some voice sounds; if he answered what I asked I didn't see how he could say anything but straight ahead.

He nodded vaguely off into the gray veils, certainly not ahead, and I said, "Well, don't you think we'd better cross? We'll be getting out into the Sound."

When he didn't say anything I began to wonder if he was drunker than I had believed; his hand had seemed steady enough as he held out the jar. I said, "Where are you taking us? Do you know where you are?"

My tone was bitter enough to make him answer, after a fashion. "Too late to cross now, Mister. It would be full dark before I got in the North Fork."

"What do you mean?" I felt almost physically sick at what he meant.

"I'm looking for Camber's Landing."

I cried out the name in a sort of reflex, signifying nothing but a sense of helplessness, and he said something about tie up for the night, Bluffton in the morning, something about he had to get gas, something about people came there fishing; I heard it all but from far off.

What I really heard was on another level, a toneless voice telling me I had passed the moment of possibility, the last seaward moment. The possible had become the impossible, the unacceptable acceptable; the hypothesis had become the dogma, having the eggs of it in itself all along. And I hadn't seen the moment as it passed. I couldn't help letting my head fall on my knees, though almost at once I was aware of a kind of mindless hope seeming to go on senselessly twitching in me, the dead snake on the road sign that wouldn't hang still until the sun went down. Acceptable perhaps, but not accepted, not yet. Couldn't there be a phone at Camber's Landing? I didn't remember any such place on the map, but people came there fishing. There might be. Suppose I got through to Graham at home (he would have left the office), gave him the whole story: conditions beyond my control, one more day's delay, only one, it goes out tomorrow without fail. Why should he be any more intransigent than if the flight had been canceled by weather? Yet I thought he would be; I thought his answer would be prompt and emphatic, partly out of simple exasperation and partly simply for the pleasure of straightening one of us out on who could push whom. All right then, how about starting it in the next number?— Still I think some corner of me did realize the moment had passed, had had the realization for an hour or more, maybe most of the day, buttoned away out of sight in the Just-in-Case pocket. "Too late" was here.

And I said okay, I miss the plane. What do I have left? Maybe some other magazine would run it, or part of it. But it might take months to find another magazine; if one could be found at all, what with different publishing schedules, different editorial tastes, different luck. To say nothing of the probable coolness in the market after Graham had worked me over at two or three cocktail parties. Okay, I've just dropped a small fortune into this black salt-smelling bay; what then? Well, I still had it as a book. Tom Dukes would go ahead with the book, disappointed no doubt but not too badly. I tested that, top and bottom, one side and another; it seemed to hold. Not everything was lost.

It was partly the comfort of that, but more than anything I think it was the rain blowing against the back of my neck that brought my head up out of this emotional display. The film of waterdrops reminded me that the manuscript, for all its importance to me, had really become a secondary matter. We were in an open boat, lost among a maze of dim creeks and inlets and estuaries; or as good as lost, I felt. Dark was coming on. Certainly I hadn't deliberately got us into all this, and yet in a way it was my fault. She said, "I'm scared. I don't like this."

I took her hand and she gripped my fingers so tightly the blisters ached through the numbness. She leaned toward my ear. "I don't think he knows where he is."

I said, "We're all right. We're still in the river. We can pull over there a hundrred yards and land any time we have to." I wasn't sure of any of it but I said it.

"Suppose we don't get out of this. Suppose he takes us out in the Sound and dumps us. He could, you know." I said firmly he wouldn't, and believed it. "One very good reason he won't is I think he needs my signature on the burial permit."

"But he knows we know about Jared."

I said, "We don't know anything about Jared. Get that out of your head. We don't know anything." I may have been saying it as much for my own benefit as hers but it was really true. The difference between us was that she wanted to know more and I didn't. There are lots of things I don't need to know; my engine has learned to operate quite well on a low-certainty octane. I thought she accepted it, or the biggest part of it, and I said to her in our half whisper, "We'll get out. Just sit tight."

"If we don't freeze to death."

"It's not so cold. It's the wind. We could turn out of the wind and it wouldn't be really cold."

"We can't land. It's nothing but mud and shells and marshgrass."

I didn't know what I could say. There comes a time when there's nothing to say.

I heard a sound then that brought up country pastures in a summer afternoon, cows waiting at a whitewashed gate, but the picture vanished in a second as I added up what the sound meant. It was a bellbuoy tilting with a drowsy liquid far-off toll, and I knew that though a bellbuoy might be in the river or the upper bay it was much more likely to be in the Sound; I figured, what with the tide running, we were farther down than we had believed. The shore had disappeared, in the darkness I had thought but I wondered now if we might not have left it behind. She heard it and when, after a time, it tolled again, a little louder, she murmured to herself or to me, in a manner that reminded me of her "breaking out the fiddle," on the highway and the island, to swallow a draft of courage, "*And*

*the ground swell, that is and was from the beginning,*
*Clangs The bell.*"

I remembered it over the years and her voice now made
of my readings a sort of chime that rang, for all its chill,
with some of the same enheartenment as the notes she had
drawn out over disappearing Jared. I wondered if she
didn't take from it the same kind of infusion, because she
went back to *The fog is in the fir trees* and recited it down
to *Clangs The bell.* And the bell clanged.

Or the bells. The one in the pasture coming up thin into
the top of the windmill clanking absent-mindedly with a
greasy softness, a good iron ladder that got a little nar-
rower as you climbed and came up under the dripping
bottom of the tank, then on up along the sides, the rungs
close against the staves so that you turned your bare foot
sideways and felt the wind and looked off to hell and gone,
the blue blades revolving above you, lifting the greasy rod,
and the bell floating up from the pasture. You come down
off of there this minute! Why? What's the matter? You
come down! I just wanted to see what's in the tank. You
come down! All right, all right. This minute! I hear you.
Lord-a-mussy, he's up on the windmill, don't look! Old
and scared of falling; you couldn't fall any more than a
squirrel could fall or a possum. And the summer-nights
bell coming in from the Army post in our town, "the
Arsenal," and the hand of a corporal in a flat-brimmed hat
with a red cord—leggings according to the era, rolled or
canvas—striking the hour, a nice variation in the man-
made intervals, and nothing to set your watch by in any
case; and sometimes on the long counts toward a drowsy
midnight thinking he had reached the end and then, after
a thoughtful space, recovering to know somehow he hadn't
and jerking the rope once again, a large bronze bell on a

twenty-foot tower. And one dreadful midnight, striking twelve and thinking it over, debating it, maybe scratching for it under the flat-brimmed hat, then deciding it and banging again, and every ear in five wards seemed to have been lying there on its pillow awake and counting—

I could feel the solid side of my box through her coat, could sense almost as plainly the solid absurdity of going through all this for so little; though of course it was no longer because of the book we were going through it but because there was no way out but through. The situation wouldn't have been the least bit different if the book had been "in your own hand"; as if such a detail were of no matter at all. And yet there would have been a copy back at the plantation, as there was of this, and if I had now unknowingly written my last book I should regret the copy wasn't of that one instead of this one; that was all the difference it would make. Unless you went along with her on the efficacy of torment. And if there was no way out but through, and no way through, this could possibly really be the end, first this morning another's, now not another's.

And I sat there looking into myself at all this, and yet hardly seeing it, until she clutched my hand. "Look! Right over there."

"What?"

"It's gone," lowering her arm from pointing off to our left as we faced up the river, or what had been the river. "I thought I saw a light."

The quickness with which the Indian cut the motor to a watery idling told me plainly enough he actually was lost. He leaped on what she said as I did, turning halfway round on his seat to stare. Whether she had seen a light or not, there was nothing now but the soft wet cloud of fog or rain or night. He said, "A light got no business being back there," continuing to look and like us continuing to look at nothing and then putting the steering handle over hard and swinging about, too far, it seemed to me, but there was nothing to gauge by except a memory of where she had been pointing, and except the change in the rain as we turned and it blew in from the side and then into our faces, seeming to slacken as he opened the throttle wider and moved with it. I slid about on the wet seat to watch for a reappearance and as she started to face about too I took the manuscript to give her more freedom with her fiddle cases and coat; the box was warm from where she had held it and I hugged it against my shirt. The light seemed to have sunk back forever into a nonexistence.

After a time the pale gray band of an oyster bank appeared, quite close beside us and moving past with an astonishing slowness considering the noise of the motor; it was obvious we had swung into the tide and though that meant burning up more gas to get anywhere I was glad to turn away from the sea. But going back the way we had come, if that was what we were doing, was no solution in itself. We hadn't seen any light as we came down. We might have missed it because of the fog; or we might have missed it from being too close in to the marsh and the thatched-roof overhang. Or we might have missed it because it wasn't there. I said, "You're sure you saw something?"

"No. But I think so," considering it a second then, "Yes, I'm sure. But I can't tell where now. We've swung round."

It seemed to me we were closer in to the bank now than when we had come down and I said to the Indian, "Why don't you pull out farther where we can get a better view?" the separated words coming out chopped-off and stiff; I could feel the wet shirt cold on my shoulders where the rain had soaked through my coat, and the wet flannel clinging over my knees. I remembered the running tide before I finished asking and I hoped he wouldn't answer, which he didn't.

Then she saw it again and grabbed my arm and I saw it too, a weak orange-colored point, not up ahead where I was watching, out over the marsh somewhere, a steady burning, not a beacon, shining with a feel of motion maybe from our own movement or from the fog drifting across it in long undulations like a ground swell and tipping it. I wondered if it really might be moving, a riding light on the mast of a boat in another fork of the river. Or rocking on a buoy. Then it was gone and he had cut the motor in indecision until we were hardly holding our own in the current; I suppose he was wondering whether to gamble on finding the right channel into the marsh by going on up the river or back down into the Sound.

I don't know what decided him (if he knew himself) but he swung about into the wind again and the tide picked us up. And I hadn't the strength or the interest to face round on the seat once more. The light was gone. And the bell was gone. And the square prow of the bateau was as good as gone, almost undiscernible in the dark. And I thought we have now begun to shift and flounder the way a pulse races and drags, drawing to an end, this enigma sitting back there at the rudder like an executioner that hadn't yet quite made up his mind how to pull it off. She said, "You know, I'm so scared, when I get out of this I don't think I'll ever be scared again, not of anything."

I noticed her young "when," strong and strength-giving against the weakling "if" on my own tongue which most of my "whens" had aged into. I didn't want to say I was scared, probably because I was more scared than she was—

with so many more years to hang scareds on—and probably because I wasn't at all sure I could even say *if* we got
out of this I wouldn't be scared again: I knew of too many
different kinds of scareds. It was one thing to be scared of
illness and pain, another to be scared of derision, another
to be scared of yourself, scared of your own shadow
(maybe the commonest one); I had known them all and I
couldn't hope to wipe the slate clean. I thought I should be
doing well to eliminate one and I wondered if, granting
deliverance, I could eliminate the last. Couldn't I honestly
say, here I am sitting in the almost dark as if resting a minute before going on into annihilation, sitting here fully
conscious on the frontier of unconsciousness, and I see now
all this has been too transient and fleeting to bother with
spending yourself on what you don't believe in? As, thirty-
two years ago, from the other end, Undergraduate Johns
saw it would be? Or was the urge to say it just part of
being scared? Well, you might be scared into doing the
right thing but it stayed the right thing just the same. If I
had a chance to talk to the guard at this chilly frontier or
the customs official or someone in authority I thought I
could say I had done things I shouldn't have and not done
things I should have, not meaning it in a religious sense but
as a mere statement of fact, and that if he would wangle
me an extension and I could go back and have a little more
time I would correct all that, or a great part of it, or at
least I would write my life in my own hand. He was cold-
eyed as only a petty official can be, black moustache that
might have been false, a rubber stamp poised to slam down
on one page or the other according to whether I was to go
on or back, a pistol in a parched holster. What was the
purpose of your visit? the accent slightly French but the
voice giving him away.—That's a hard question, Dr. Mole.

—Pleasure? Fun? The pursuit of happiness, I reckon.—Not entirely. I wanted to go places, write about them, about the people I saw, how they looked to me.—Looks like you didn't get very far. Looks like they give you a lot more visas than you could find any use for.—I couldn't get everywhere I wanted to go, that's what I'd like to talk to you about.—Looks like you spent most of your time girl-watching on the rue de Rivoli.—No. I did a good deal of real work too. I just got sidetracked there for a while.—That box you've got wrapped up there in all that wet paper, is that some fancy French postcards you're taking home?—Not exactly, and I was just about to throw it in the river anyhow. If you can arrange for me to return I'm ready now to get on with what I started out to do way back thirty years ago.—That's what everybody says. Chances are you'd end up on a café terrace right where you were before. Same chair.—No, it's different now.—The difference is you're scared now.—No, that's just part of it. That's not the whole thing.—You see the light now, I reckon.—Yes I do, I see the light.—How many lights do you see?—You seem to be making fun of me, Doctor, but I do see the light. Three or four lights.—And now you want to stand up on your own feet, you've been sitting down so long?—That's it. Yes I do. I've been sitting here so long my knees are frozen.—Maybe they're too frozen to stand up on.—No, I can stand up.—Stand up straight before your own name?—Yes, I can do that.—Your name is Bill, I believe.—No. Wesley. Wesley Johns.—You see the light, Wesley?

He bumped the stamp down so hard on one of the pages (I couldn't tell which) it almost knocked me out of the boat.

"Are you all right, Wesley?"

156

"What's all this?"

The black pilings of the dock rose up over us, the bottoms chattering like a cage of rats with the tide drawing away through the crust of barnacles. A man in a yellow raincoat, on his knees against the light, was gazing down on us pointing a flashlight at a slimy ladder on the second pile. I could see the tough fat hull of a shrimp boat ahead of us, *Ibis II*, bolt heads caked with rust, a hank of net looping down from a spar, ropes gleaming in the wet, great slabs of mud-smelling blackness where the lights expired.

"Isn't this the most beautiful, beautiful, beautiful!" she flung her arms about me like a damp bear.

The man on the dock said, aiming the flashlight, "Ain't that Luke Mole?" and Luke said, "You look awful pretty to me, Al," shutting off the idling motor, the quiet like a soft seal authenticating we were there. She ran both palms backward over her head, pressing the water from her hair, gathering the dank strings from beside her face.

The ladder felt warm against my cold fingers as I held the boat against it while she stood up, grasped it and climbed it, surefooted and easy, as if recalling treehouses and haylofts, crawling out on the dock floor in a huge ball of arms and legs and mist-covered overcoat and reaching down on all fours. She asked for the viola and I passed it up and then passed up the violin, balancing the ends in two stiff hands so numb I stood there looking at the dark shapes being lifted on up half thinking I still had hold of them. "Okay, now give me the manuscript."

It had slipped off the seat where I had laid it and was canted against the side in the dim light, an edge in a little water sluicing the bottom. I got it, brushed at it dismally with the side of my palm, caught my stick-fingers on the cord and knocked it out of my hands; it hit the gunwale flat, flipped over and splashed. My hands, wrists, coat sleeves, upper arms plunged in after it. I touched it, felt the knot, the paper slick with water, the ragged corner. It wasn't sinking very fast, tumbling about weightless as a child's balloon, but I couldn't get under it with any grip or round it, couldn't get my fingers through the cord, the boat rocking, my face nearly in the water, the hat floating away. I almost hooked it once with the joint of my first finger, arm's length down in the thick blackness, but it twisted free.

# SEVEN

The sunlight was in a dry yellow
square on the wall of a high bare room the first time I
opened my eyes; the next time it had moved far down into
a long slant across a threadbare rug, a shaft of blue dust
motes floating like worlds in the Milky Way beyond the
iron-and-brass scrolls in the foot of the bed; the last time
it had drawn close to the sill of a floor-to-ceiling window
giving on to a porch, upstairs, from the bend of the tree
branches I could see. In between the times I seemed to be
tumbling about, weightless like the box, in a past-present
that was altogether strange to me, strange to my opened
eyes looking back on it, though to my closed, looking into
it, I felt completely at home, as if I had been there before
in some deeper level of awareness but had been unable to
bring out any of it with me, a past-present that had to be
mine, however irreconcilable, because it could be nobody
else's, vivid, endlessly varied, fresh, unworn, unaged, un-
wearied, and none of it carrying any questions for me of
where this sunwashed room was or how I got there—which
I seemed to know well enough without caring to bother

at the moment with bringing it up for an overt answer—other questions pressing in ahead of them about the images themselves, what their parentage was and how they had got into me and what others were there behind them that hadn't yet come forward? all of it full of some implication that I couldn't put my finger on about who was I after all? If a man couldn't account for such things as these, how reliable was his measure of himself then? as if his measure of himself were no more to be relied on than mine had been of this day, standing there contentedly counting nine on the courthouse clock, my eyes now falling shut again and myself falling back into the unaccountable presence of four young men crowding me into a corner, one with a bale hook, one tapping me softly on the mouth with a pair of pliers, and all breaking up suddenly as the threat becomes unbearable, I with the hook and throwing it away into a passing wagon and walking off into a house that is being torn down. And Josephine, beautiful and coming toward me on stilts about eight feet high and managing them so well you can't see them under her stockings.

On into a sharp dread of having to change trains at a country junction smelling of turpentine, waiting for the new train with a blanket roll, several bottles of Coca-Cola, a box of paper, an icepick, one train after another shooting through. I am shaving and a pleasant train of one observation car running under its own power stops and Livia calls to me this is our train. A frantic attempt to get my things aboard in one trip, throwing what I can on the platform of the car, the conductor fingering his watch, impatient to go, and I back for more baggage, which by now has accumulated so that taking it all is obviously hopeless, and I am half inclined, breathless and unable to move quickly, to let the train go rather than leave so much behind, bottles and jars, a shotgun, two yellow boats, the yellow coming up much brighter now and in a square and becoming the sunlight on the west wall of the room.

A fly-specked light bulb on a wire with a take-up loop in it was hanging from the center of the ceiling, longtime symbol for me of the utterly forlorn, and I turned over in the crackling bed to get away from it and followed raised street car tracks in a muddy road out toward a baseball park.

With Livia in a shaky brown station wagon getting gas at a crowded handpump in Naylor then beside a country road under repairs, half a dozen black sleek mules, one of them ours. I ask Cloud if he will feed the mule for me, then tell Livia to go get the mule, her face changing, she isn't keen for the job, as neither am I. I go alone, bringing the mule back in my arms, heavy but not as heavy as I expected, not as bad a job. Cloud asks what I feed him but I don't know. 'Just the regular thing. He hasn't eaten since yesterday morning,' then thinking this sounds as if we don't take care of our livestock, 'or maybe yesterday noon,' telling the story of how we happen to be there to a number of people not much interested, one of them the proprietor of a fancy restaurant. I try to tell Carlotta on a stool at the bar but she won't listen and the proprietor in black orders me a drink on the house in a wide-top jar and I explain in earnest I know something to his advantage, very important, his attention wandering as he speaks right and left, not caring, just waiting for me to get it off my chest. And I am in a car going at high speed on a misty road in the mountains, Carlotta driving, close to the edge several times then straight on over a round green cliff when the road swings out from under, the sun shining up in my eyes, a jukebox going.

And I came out of it enough to see that the sun had moved round to where it was striking the brass ball on the bedpost, the room warm and dry and full of light, a radio coming up into the silence from downstairs, no street noises outside, no traffic, then the single beep of a motor horn and I am riding in a bus through the streets of a city, the outskirts, a large city that I know by maps I have seen before, know how the streets will cross a wide river, the Ohio. Not many on the bus, not much traffic, winding on and I watching, curious but feeling symptoms of a growing depression at the place; then up a ramp and I brace myself to see the great river, which I need to see, then over a dike and down, no river but rows of handsome houses, gray stone, columns, arches, all empty, a line cutting through them marking the height of the last flood.

Then a redheaded man is squatting beside me as I kneel by a pipe fence. He says there has been some mistake, the head man has sent word he never received my invention. 'What do I do?' 'He's got it now. You just have to wait ten more days.' I feel put upon, but what can you do? On the other side of the fence Graham comes up a slope with a large box on his shoulder, turns off beyond calling distance, and I go into a bar and ask for a case of Miller's, huge plates going by piled with food, thick slices of roast beef medium-rare one on another, corn, potatoes, something like sauerkraut or beans. I tell the waiter I only want the roast beef; he seems surprised and I am affected, ashamed to be. 'Oh give me some potatoes too.' Before I can eat it the people I am with are ready to move on and I am at a high desk asking for my bill. 'I only had the roast beef.' Two waiters search the records and at last one brings me a small thin ticket divided in the middle as if to be torn, like a theater ticket but flimsy, small print showing two luncheons at twenty-three dollars. I am indignant. They explain that the regular lunch is seven dollars but with the special one I ordered it naturally runs a little higher; besides, everything is going up. I am disgusted, tempted to pay and get out but hating to be fleeced, the mirror behind the bar becoming a scrubbed blue sky beyond a sunny window and everything fading into it and gone like the ice-blue blimp trailing its F-sharp buzz and its mooring cables without a mooring.

And I lifted my head and studied where they had been, images that had had nothing to do with any me that I knew, nothing in them that I recognized beyond a few details that didn't matter, an ocean depth with fishes of every kind and corals and serpents and man-eating sharks all leading a life of their own not meant for the light of day, and gone now, trailing behind them nothing much more than a half-felt freshening, a sense of someone that was not the self I accepted as I but as valid, as true, the dark of the moon that was no less true for being dark, a sense of forgotten strengths no less real for being forgotten. All of it gone into the sky as I studied it, then studied my empty wrist for the time, then my bare arm and chest and the rest of me bare under the coarse sheet and blanket, then sat bolt upright in the conviction I had been robbed, watch gone, clothes, shoes. Manuscript? Manuscript gone.

"Jo!"

And I was back in reality, sitting on the sodden planks of the dock, teeth chattering, muscles fluttering, nerves shaking with what had happened, listening to her ask the man in the yellow raincoat if there was a doctor in the town. "I don't need a doctor," pulling myself together and getting up to prove it, the gray-white mist sliding endlessly across the floodlight. "Is there some place here we can spend the night? Boarding house? Rooms?"

"Hotel, Mister. Binnion's Hotel. Old man Binnion's dead, *been* dead. Mrs. Inglett runs it now."

I cut him short to ask how we got there and he said, "Right there, end the dock," in a voice that squeaked like a sea bird. "Big house, double porches, you'll see it. Binnion's Hotel. Other side Earl Copus's garage." He turned away to take the barrel of the shotgun sticking out of the dark, calling down, "Ain't got but one gun, Luke?" as if we had been out duck hunting.

She said, "Come on, you'll get pneumonia," grabbed my wet arm and pulled me unresisting into a dim interminable walk down the glistening boards—spars and low masts beside us, rigging, nets like skeins of moss, the black funnel of a "Boat for Hire," *Nancy, Capt. Hammersmith,* shacks and tin sheds packed with the smell of crabs and shrimp, yellow light after yellow light coming out of the mist, passing above us scratched with rain, sinking into the mist behind. Once she said, "You had me worried for a while, Wesley."

I mumbled I had myself worried. "I'm not all over it."

"I don't mean that. I mean the manuscript."

I groaned, speechless at the thought (half wondering too if the kid was mad enough to believe I had destroyed my book on purpose), and she said never mind as if seeing now was no time to bring that up, and there was the feel of crushed shells underfoot in place of the boards, and then a warehouse, the garage that would have meant everything once and meant nothing now as things have a way of doing, the lighted window of a drugstore, and then the double porches and Mrs. Inglett in a rocking chair at a television screen. Through a door beyond the stairs a large colored woman was drying dishes at a kitchen sink.

"D'e fall in the river!" talking past me, as if I were a halfwit patient.

Which I almost was, quivering, wanting nothing so much as to get out of the cold blanket that seemed to envelop me like an outer skin. My brain felt as gelid as my fingers, drifting stiffly round a phone booth by the stairs and a shadowy admonition that I had better do something about Graham and on into a vision of how it would be to have pneumonia in Binnion's Hotel, Mrs. Inglett behind the high desk now, unscrewing the top from a bottle of ink and taking a pen out of a drawer and handing it to Jo.

We followed her up the bare steps to a wide hall furnished with some skewed wicker chairs, a flat-armed sofa of the Morris-chair era, a table with torn magazines, two or three dismal light bulbs on cords from the high ceiling. Heat from downstairs had warmed the hall but the room she unlocked was full of a chill that seemed different from outside only in the wadded motionless smell of the long-closed bedroom. "It'll warm up, Honey. Leave the door open a few minutes, nobody up here. Bathroom end of the hall." A bent electric heater began to develop a wan glow.

They pulled off my clothes, as indifferent to my shuddering white body as if I had been a department-store manikin, some thin layer of my brain telling me I was humiliated—at the stripping itself and also at the weak shaking it revealed—but most of me failing to register anything, not caring, preoccupied with the job of trying to hold my chest and shoulders quiet, as though believing I could save myself a chill if I put my mind to it. Mrs. Inglett hung a not-too-clean patchwork quilt about me and backed me to the bed like a horse, bending me in the middle and sitting me down.

They were taking off my shoes, one to each, when the colored woman appeared in the door with an earthenware teapot and cups on a tray and a small red-brown can by the cups stamped with a bee in flight and *Busy Bee Snuff.* "Indian Luke's been here, Miss Cora, says tell the young missus here's some medicine for her to give him." I said snuff! and she said, "No sir, ain't snuff. Says stir it all in a cup of tea and drink it down." Mrs. Inglett told her (O.C., maybe Osie) to put some hominy and shrimp on the back of the stove; we could get it when we were ready. Food didn't interest me but I said the young lady would be down.

When they had gone, dividing my clothes and shoes and the great khaki overcoat between them, Jo set the tray on a chair by the bed and poured two cups of tea. I said I wished it was a good slug of whiskey and she said he must have drunk all the booze himself, then "Mrs. What's-her-name must have some whiskey." She picked up a towel from the washstand and went out drying her hair, barefoot now moving without a sound on the old straw rugs, the blue dress streaked with dark about the hem.

The effect on me, or what was left of me, of her going was to leave me, not so much alone as alone with the Busy Bee snuffbox, with all the complicated things that were in it besides the "medicine." My first response had been to dismiss without a thought the idea of taking it; I don't think she looked at the idea long enough to dismiss it. She brushed it to a corner of the tray with the back of her hand while she poured the tea. Neither of us opened it or shook it or weighed it. But as I drank some of the tea, which I didn't want, and lay down, shoulders vibrating like the bateau with the motor going, I saw it sitting there and began to see a lot else, not seeing with any enumerating consciousness, which my brain seemed incapable of anyhow, but seeing in little shafts of illumination like

166

walking with a flashlight. If I took Luke Mole's prescription and did not end up like Jared I should really be cured not only of worrying about the doctor's guilt and my own gratuitous involvement in it but of carrying round with me the rest of my life the idea that I had lacked the courage to accuse him because it would have been accusing myself too. Not that this would be a conclusive proof of anything, but mightn't it be enough of a weight in the scales, not much out of balance now, to tip them over the other way? The faith in him necessary to take his medicine spread on beyond that into other things about him too.

Perhaps I shouldn't have argued this way with a clear mind, though it seemed clear enough at the time, particularly clear in fact. And perhaps also underneath my consciousness was the safety-belt thought of the man in the raincoat calling his name, of his being known in Mrs. Inglett's kitchen. I mean, drinking the stuff, which ordinarily I probably wouldn't have done, was not really such a quixotic thing to do; I had reasons for doing it and reasons for thinking it would be all right.

I don't know what bog or fernbrake or moldy stump or livid brew it came out of but I poured it all, a yellow-brown powder, about half a jigger of it, into the teacup, stirred it a minute until it disappeared and downed it. My misgivings mounted up in a swell at the shocking taste of it—the uncomfortable picture returning to me, as my chest almost immediately began to steady, of the trestle table under the gum tree and the wide-mouth jars of heaven knows what—and I mixed an inch or so of tea with cream and sugar and swallowed that. Then I capped the can with the flying bee, set it back innocently in the corner behind the teapot ,and that was the end of the day for me.

I woke in the night, or half woke, to the sound of someone quietly breathing, stared about in the dimness, something saying to me that this was what I had asked for, wasn't it? and I denying it (the light had been turned off but there was a filtered illumination from somewhere); I studied the shape of a face on the other pillow that I couldn't account for though the triangle of white teeth seemed somehow reassuring, then sank back into the unfamiliar depths I had just come out of where I was saying, "Now by this I know that the word in thy mouth is truth," an old man with moss on his chin who called himself Elijah handing me up out of a grave, or a flood, to a woman who thanked him with a triangular smile and pulled me up a wet vertical ladder into a zone of light.

My watch was on the bureau, wallet, money, cigarettes, keys, glasses; everything seemed to be there. I didn't count the money but it looked all right. The watch had stopped, but from the position the sunlight had moved into I guessed it was afternoon, two or three o'clock. The tray was gone with the tea things, the busy bee was gone, and as it came back to me clearly how she had stood the fiddle cases side by side in the angle of the bureau and the wall I saw that they were gone too. The thought that jumped into my mind hung there for only a second; she couldn't have left me because I had her suitcase locked up in the car.

The hall was in half light and colder than the room now with the dry sun flooding into it; a few squawks of a popular song drifted up the stairwell and died off into a jabber of radio talk. I wrapped the quilt round me and went to the banisters and called her and then Mrs. Inglett and then I went down far enough to lean over and see into the kitchen and called, "Osie! Cook!" In a break of the radio chatter I managed to get her attention.

She brought up my clothes, the shirt and underclothes on a folded newspaper clean and ironed, the coat and trousers pressed, shoes brushed. She gazed at me hard, smiling a little. "You look like you feeling better."

I said born again.

She said dinner was over but she could give me some soda-biscuits and shrimp and rice and some fresh-baked chocolate pie. "You must be hungry, no supper. I've got a nice pompano if you tired of shrimp."

I listened for a second to the echoes of "pompano" and took the shrimp. I said "Have you seen the young lady?"

"The young missus she was up early. Waiting for breakfast when I come."

I said I would be down in a few minutes. "If you see the young lady tell her I'm up. At last. Tell her we'll be leaving in half an hour or so." As she started down the stairs I said, "And will you tell Mrs. Inglett?" She said Miss Cora had gone up to the post office but she would tell her as soon as she got back.

I considered taking a bath, decided if there was one thing I didn't want any more of at the moment it was water and, with a minimum of washing, got into my smooth kitchen-scented clothes. She met me at the foot of the stairs with my tray of breakfast-lunch-dinner, whatever it was, and I had her take it to a sofa by a south window and sat down with my shoulders in the sun as if I could never get enough of it. Outside, Mrs. Inglett had an enclosed garden full of parrots and parakeets, three or four small monkeys with faces like tennis balls, and I listened to them as I ate, all chattering and squealing and swinging in the sun. I was hungry; I enjoyed everything until my eye fell on the phone booth and the questions chattering and squealing and swinging about it. After that I hardly knew what I was eating.

Where was I this morning, this sunny afternoon, with an afternoon's beard on my cheeks? Graham over there against the side of stairs, and Tom Dukes too, and all the rest of the level-headed world, the common-sense yesterday world. And over here a visionary young woman and a temerarious old man on the point of making a fool of himself, if he hadn't already done it. What about the carbon I had at the plantation? What about this girl? Appearing out of nowhere like a sudden answer you have forgotten you asked for; leading me out of hell in a sort of upside-down Orpheus-Eurydice, out of the labyrinth by a thread that was almost my own thread, or had been once. What about myself? Led out for once and all, or just until I came to my senses? I could forget the magazine; I was willing to be that much of a fool—it being unavoidable anyway now—but what about the rest of it? What did I say to Graham? Or if I ducked out of that one, as I might, and called Tom Dukes instead, what did I say? My hands were half frozen, old man, and I just dropped the damned thing, that's all, and when I tried to recover it in the water it got away, I almost had it once, all right, I did have it, and something got into me, you see I'd been thinking a lot about this job all day, in fact, Tom, I'll tell you, I'll be frank with you, I ran into this kid Eurydice, no, I mean—

I threw the napkin in a corner of the sofa and got up. All I knew for certain was that I was a long way from yesterday, a long way from justifying myself, as someone had said, noisily and with gestures like a lawyer trying to put something over on himself, a long way from cocky telegrams, cocky anything. I didn't know where I was, but not back there. Maybe something could be worked out.

Maybe it couldn't. I'd have to decide that on the basis of a new position—that wasn't entirely new, with its bearings and its props footing back, not into yesterday, but into thirty years ago and purple cinders on college steps, and beyond that, even, to my father's voice and Remember now thy Creator in the days of thy youth, and beyond.— What about holding this thing up, Tom? Let's think about it a little bit.—It's your book, Bill.—I feel like a fool to say it, Tom, and I hope the hell you won't laugh but I'd like to put out something better than this, try to anyhow, if I can't I can't but you might as well give yourself the benefit of the doubt. I mean it doesn't pay to be in too big a hurry to accept your limitations.—Are you all right, Bill? You feeling all right?—I'm fine. I tell you, Tom, let's think about this thing and I'll phone you, what's today? Is today Friday? Thursday? I couldn't say what today was. I thought for me it was a day with an eighth name, yesterday in a flow of events beyond my control, and now up again into control, or a certain degree of control—

"Good morning, Mrs. Inglett." We talked for a minute, she calling me "Mr. Wesley," about the sunlight and how we were feeling, I hating to greet her pointblank with the question that was on my mind.

It turned out I didn't have to ask it, for while we were talking she went behind the desk and fished down an envelope out of pigeonhole Number Three. "Mrs. Wesley left you a note, said you would understand. Said your car keys were in here too."

I said I had my car keys, taking out the little leather jacket I carried them in and unsnapping it and seeing that I didn't, and beginning to grasp that something was wrong.

"And this other thing," handing it all to me. The "other thing" was a pitchpipe.

I said, "Where is she?"

"She got back with your car about ten-thirty. It's right there by the porch, didn't you see it? Earl Copus went with her, fixed it, flat or something. She said you'd pay him."

I said I'd pay him all right, where was she? And Mrs. Inglett said, "She told me Earl was going into town and would give her a lift. I said, 'Honey, what do you want me to tell Mr. Wesley about where to find you?' And she said give you this. What's the matter? You don't mean she walked out on you?"

I said oh no. Of course not. Some such thing. I'm not sure what I said. I took the note over to the window; I can still read without glasses if the light is good. There wasn't much to read. *Most wonderful hitch. Most wonderful gesture.* And I now saw, scratched on the back of the envelope in an afterthought, *The pitchpipe is for piping the pitch.* Mrs. Inglett had four canaries in an oblong cage that she had set out in the sun, or the cook had, since I had looked earlier; they were whistling and swinging with all the rest and I watched them for a few minutes through the glass.

I called The West Green and the desk put me through to the orchestra leader. When he found out what I wanted he turned mean. He had had a wire from her she wasn't taking the job. "What did she say?" "*That's* what she said." "Now listen!" "You tell that woman from me—" I hung up.

I drove into the town, Sessoms, about five miles on a dirt road across the creeks and marshes and five more on a blacktop through the pines. I asked at the two filling stations (she was easy enough to identify), in the drugstore, in the newsstand-lunch counter where the bus stopped, in a cheap café; there was no hotel. An old colored man warming his shoulders against the sunny bricks of the hardware store on a corner where the four-lane sliced through the town had seen her climb into the cab of a long-haul truck headed south. And she was gone and not gone, the viola sounds, and every sound and thought and feeling that went with them, ringing in my ears all the way back to the plantation, all the time I was reading the message to call Mr. Dukes urgent and waiting for the call to go through, all the way to Chapel Hill and the University. And ringing still, for that matter.